ORIONS GATE: TEAM GALAXY RIDERS

THE GREAT SPACE RACE

SABINE PRIESTLEY

KAC PUBLISHING

FOREWORD

Welcome to The Great Space Race! We hope you enjoy this collection of stories from best selling and award winning authors of Sci-Fi Romance!

You can find the entire series of books, all of which stand alone perfectly well, here: https://gspacerace.com/

CHAPTER 1

*A*rmond Nolde extended his psi beyond the realm of known space. Farther than he'd ever gone before, but the exact distance eluded him. He'd been experimenting with the limits of the distorters for the past few months, and had been surprised to find that his range increased with practice. It presented a fascinating question of precisely how far he could go. Ever cautious of his own limits with control, he stilled his mind and expanded farther. Something was different this time. Wrong.

An odd sensation etched its way along his psi, and trickled down his spine. Energized. Foreign. Increasing in strength.

His head spun, and he reached out for the table in front of him, only to find nothing as his body was propelled forward.

He was in a portal.

Drawing on years of experience, he clamped down his fear and analyzed the situation. There was no mistaking the fact he was intra-portal, but he hadn't initiated a jump. And, as far as he knew, there was no distorter on the other end. As with any portal transit, his vision was severely affected, but the color hues were not the usual muted purples and blues. A brighter yellow existed, something he'd never seen before. More disturbing was the duration of the jump. The longest one had lasted perhaps three seconds; he had to be pushing fifteen at this point.

He tried to pull back his psi, but he was inexplicably anchored on the other end. Had he gone too far? What if he was in this state indefinitely? Would his body deteriorate? Did it need air, nutrition, in the void that was interstellar portal space?

It was a fascinating proposition. He sensed the termination coming a split second before he slammed into a cold, hard surface, his head making a sickening crunch on impact. Stars exploded and pain shot through his forehead and down his left arm.

He rolled to his back, suppressing a moan of pain. Taking a deep breath he evaluated his body while waiting for his vision to return. Aside from his head and arm, he appeared to be uninjured, but a concussion was likely. He probed his forehead with his right hand and found a large welt, slick with blood.

He'd been holding the distorter when the portal opened, but his hands were empty now.

There was movement nearby, and something was pressed against his right ear. A quick prod found a small ear piece had been inserted. "Who's there?"

2

A gravelly woman's voice spoke, but it made no sense.

The surface on which he lay was cool and hard under his fingers. Light filtered into his blurred vision, but patches of grey were all he could see.

He reached out with his psi and found another entity. It was a different psi than he'd experienced before, which meant there were now three unique types in the galaxy. He had no idea what the implications were of that.

A scratching sound came from his left. Familiar, somehow. A breath expelled. Slowly, he differentiated a shadow, movement to accompany the noise.

"Oh it's definitely humanoid," the woman said, "and deliciously male, but I've never seen one with this coloring before. I've fitted him with a translator. We'll see if he's able to process it." The voice had an irritating sing-song quality. "Large, muscled, and rather delightful looking. I hope he responds to treatment; he'll make an excellent contestant. I do love this part." The sound of hands clapping. "What do you have?"

A faint voice, barely audible. Male.

"Feline? Really? Can't wait to see that. The pairings are always such fun. How are the others doing? Anyone check-in on the forum yet?"

Pause.

"As soon as I establish communication and get the papers completed, I'll sign in. Talk to you later." Another sound, like ice rattling in a glass.

Where the gods was he?

"How are you feeling?"

He turned his head to the voice, suppressing a groan of pain. "Are you addressing me?"

"Excellent, the translator is working. It can take a while. And yes, of course I'm addressing you."

Armond blinked a few more times as focus returned. A

smallish mature woman with black and white hair sticking out in all directions, she sat on a plush bench that extended seamlessly from the wall. She wore a fuchsia-colored suit. Hem above the knee and plunging neckline. The scratching sound was a nail file as she rapidly shaped her tips.

The room was small, white, and brightly lit from above. The only furniture, the bench upon which the woman sat. "Where am I?"

"I'm asking the questions for now, and I asked how you were feeling."

Cradling his left arm, he pushed up to a sitting position. A wave of nausea washed over him. "I've been worse. I may have sustained a fracture, and probably a mild concussion."

"You did land rather spectacularly. Came through at an angle. Quite the sight." The woman placed the nail file into a black purse resting next to her. She touched a small jewel encrusted device on her right ear. He guessed it was the same as the one he wore, minus the stones. "I need a medic in three." She crossed her legs and laced her fingers over her knee.

He stared at her face as she spoke, and it took him a moment to realize that her lips didn't match the words he heard. It must be the translator in his ear.

"Can you stand?"

Armond didn't reply, simply got to his feet. The nausea passed quickly, but his head pounded. A quick scan of his surroundings confirmed the fact that his transporter was missing. "I'd like to know where I am. And how you managed to locate, intercept, and transport me." He nearly said abduct.

A high-pitched laugh emanated from lips that matched her suit. "You are delectable."

It appeared he was being detained, but the woman did not seem hostile, nor a threat.

A door on the far side of the room slid open and a chest-height blue android rolled in. The woman waved her hand at Armond. She did that a lot. "I'd like a full workup, but start with his head and left arm. He may have damaged them coming through."

"As you wish." The voice was human-like, but oddly asexual.

Armond backed up when the thing approached. He didn't like the look of the probe extending from a center compartment.

"Oh don't be silly. It won't hurt you. In fact, its programming wouldn't allow it to hurt anyone. Any organic living thing, to be more precise. You're perfectly safe."

He had no reason to trust this woman, but considering he was unarmed, his distorter missing, and he didn't know where he was, there didn't appear to be an alternative. He remained still as the droid scanned him from head to toe.

"He has a laceration and minor concussion, as well as a hairline fracture on the left humerus. Please remain still," the droid said. Another compartment opened on the body, and a palm-sized rectangle emerged. It had a semi-transparent surface that glowed blue. Starting at his elbow, it slowly moved upward. A mild burning sensation trickled between his elbow and shoulder. The process took nearly ten minutes, but when it finished, Armond was impressed to find his arm fully functional and pain free.

The droid's appendage extended farther as it held the panel close to the laceration on his head. The sensations repeated, and the intriguing thing was, unlike Sandarians, there did not appear to be any psi involved in the healing.

"I'm curious as to the technology you employed just now," Armond said when the process was complete.

The bot ignored his comment, so he looked to the woman.

She shrugged. "Go ahead and tell him."

"The panel is a molecular manipulator. It has the ability to rearrange, or in this case knit together, physical components."

Armond would love to dissect the technology. The potential for destruction, however, was disturbing. That which could heal so effectively could also redistribute molecular matter. That was nightmare material.

"You are mildly dehydrated. Drink." The droid extended a glass container. "It is water with alkaline and electrolytes."

Armond took the liquid and smelled it before tasting. It appeared to, in fact, be water.

The woman inspected him openly. "Are there more like you where you come from?"

"More like what?"

"You're all...pale." She flicked her polished nails. "Even your eyes barely have any color. I've never seen a humanoid like you. You are humanoid, I presume?"

"That is correct. I'm what is known as an albino. I lack a particular enzyme which is responsible for pigmentation."

She frowned. "Does that affect you in any other way? You appear quite strong and healthy."

"It can, but we have technology to negate any potential defects. Why?"

"Because, dear boy, I need you at your best. You are going to be my next champion. I can feel it in my labia."

Armond nearly choked on his drink.

The woman was perfectly serious. Best to leave that one alone.

The droid finished its inspection. "The specimen is fit for participation."

Specimen?

The woman stood with a burst of energy. "I had a good feeling about today."

"Participation in what?"

"You have been selected to participate in our contest. Completely voluntary of course. It is however, the only way that you will be able to return to your own galaxy. Minor detail, really."

"My own *galaxy*?"

"Yes. You are in the Paragon Galaxy. More specifically you're on Primaera, capital of the Central Alliance. Your galaxy has yet to go intergalactic so I wouldn't bother trying to find your own way home."

He detected no trace of duplicity, not in her vocal range, her physicality or her psi. The thought was staggering. But then he remembered Marco and Zara, his fellow Earth Protector and his soon to be psi-mate. They'd tried to convince him of something that sounded like a quantum temporal distortion. If it were true. Time travel in effect. He hadn't believed it at the time. Marco was known for his boyish persona and wasn't above pranks. According to them, he and a woman had come from another galaxy from three months in the future. That had been two and a half months ago. Perhaps this was just an elaborate hoax?

But that wouldn't explain how he'd just been healed without psi. Or the woman's unique form of energy. No. He had to assume this was precisely what it seemed. Extraordinary as it was. "Without my distorter, I can't go anywhere."

"You wouldn't be able to go anywhere with your little trinket. Not without my assistance. I will gladly provide both after you have completed the competition. Win, and I'll even make sure you return to where you started. All completely voluntary, of course."

She had a cunning look in her eye, and nothing about this was voluntary.

"What exactly must I do?"

"Right now, all you have to do is sign our participation

7

form and, of course, the release of liability in case of an accident, injury, or death. And dismemberment, but that rarely happens. It's usually an all-or-nothing kind of thing. It's all standard, I assure you."

"You want me to agree to something before I know what it is?"

"That's one way of putting it. Another is that we are allowing you to participate in an event that will possibly change your life forever. The potential for endorsement if you place, not to mention if you win, are astronomical. You'll be able to afford the latest spacecraft. Imagine returning to your little galaxy in possession of technology never before seen in your worlds!"

If he survived. "And if I say no?"

Her face crumpled into a pout. "That wouldn't be any fun. And I'm afraid you would find it extremely difficult, well, impossible really, to find your way back to your world. Now, be a good boy and do let's sign those papers." She pulled a com-sized device from her purse and a hologram materialized in front of them.

Armond reached out and scrolled the virtual document. There was eighteen pages of small text. It was full of legalese. The basic principal was at the very end.

Participant will not hold the Corporation liable in the event of any personal loss, injury, death, or dismemberment.

They needed eighteen pages to say that? "There is nothing in here about returning me to the Milky Way."

"The what?"

"My galaxy."

"How quaint. We don't do addendums."

"Then give me your word." He found the woman highly distasteful.

She waved her hand. "Yes, of course, of course. You have my word."

He resented being coerced, but under the circumstances, it could be far worse. They'd healed him. After abducting him. He was weaponless, and didn't know the environment. Best to go along with it for now. "How do I sign?"

The high-pitched laugh burst from her lips. She swiped the document sideways on the last page, and the outline of a palm print appeared. "Simply place your hand in the center there, and state your legal name. Oh, dear me. I haven't introduced myself yet. I'm Candice Overtop, but you can call me Candi. With an 'I.' I'll be your handler for the duration of the contest. You and your teammate, that is."

"My teammate?" And surely that wasn't her real name?

"Yes, of course. You didn't think you'd be expected to do this on your own, did you?"

"Given that I know nothing about what you expect of me, I wouldn't know."

"Well, now that we have the formalities out of the way, let's go find out who your partner is.

CANDI WALKED A FEW STEPS IN FRONT OF ARMOND. SHE barely came to his chest, and the way she moved reminded him of the Earth fowl called a goose. The environment suggested a large corporation. Many of the people they passed wore a shirt emblazoned with an emblem containing a lightning bolt and stars. Letters circled the design, but he couldn't get close enough to read them.

Candi wasn't the only one fascinated by his appearance. Nearly everyone studied him. There was a wide variety of life forms here. Perhaps they were in a spaceport then, and not a corporation. So far there had been no external windows, so it was impossible to say. He didn't detect the hum of space, but they clearly had more advanced technology, so that wasn't necessarily an accurate way to determine location. His lack of information was frustrating.

"You don't talk much, do you?" Candi said over her shoulder.

"I speak when I have something to say." It had been a while since Armond had been around strangers who didn't already know his personality. He'd yet to meet another who's intellect matched his own, and found most conversations dull and lacking substance. Perhaps this new galaxy would provide a greater intellectual challenge. If the woman in front of him was an indication, it didn't bode well.

"Here we are." Candi waved her hand, and a door slid to the side.

He followed her into a large, stark room with tiered benches lining the walls. Everything appeared to be made of grey metal, and there wasn't a seam anywhere. He wondered at the manufacturing process to produce the effect. There were a dozen or more people scattered around the room. Not all of them human.

"Come, have a seat over here. I need to go register you. We should have everyone present within the hour." She spun and left him alone. He climbed to the top of the nearest riser for the optimal view, and sat with his back to the wall. He found being without his com, or any connection to a network, unsettling.

He took his time analyzing each individual. There were a number of humans, or humanoids, present. One of the females had a fascinating resemblance to Earth's felines. Pointy ears poked through black wavy hair. He wasn't sure, but that might be a tail curled up next to her. Or maybe a pet of some kind.

Her head whipped around and she met his gaze.

Her eyes were indeed shaped like those of a cat, and almost completely green with little or no white. He wanted to get a closer look, but he'd be better served by continuing his assessment. Perhaps she would be his partner in this fiasco.

Was she the woman Marco and Zara had referred to? The thought surprised him. They didn't know that his finding a psi-mate was an impossibility, so he'd stopped them before they could describe the woman. Perhaps that had been a mistake, but if it had been a temporal distortion, the course of events would play themselves out, regardless of what he knew. In theory.

The cat woman didn't appear the least bit bothered by his staring. In fact, she smiled at him. Those teeth were evolved for eating prey, not grazing. She became more interesting by the moment. He wondered if she had claws. Given her other traits, it seemed likely. Certainly someone to keep an eye on, if nothing else.

A sapphire-skinned woman was guided into the room next. Medium height, curvy, with black hair, her skin shone a deep blue. It was difficult to tell if it was reflecting the lights or had an internal source. The woman walked with a sharp, energized gait, and sat next to a group of three others, one of whom had similar coloring. Her voice carried across the room. It had a breathy quality, but also a vocal anomaly. It was as though there were three or four of her speaking at once, with ever-so-slight pitch variations. He wondered at the physiology that could produce such an effect. Multiple vocal chords, perhaps?

The woman used her whole body when she spoke, gesturing with every sentence. The group burst into laughter at something she'd said.

The other with her coloring, a male, had the same vocal oddity. The laughter was particularly melodic.

People were filing in with increasing frequency. A short creature with four arms ambled in next. It had both male and female qualities about it, but not every species was gendered. Like the Torogs in his own universe, nothing about that race mirrored humanoids and their male-female dichotomy.

At least, if he didn't make it back to Earth and the Cavacents, he wouldn't be lacking for stimulating intellectual fodder. Still, he wanted to communicate with Lord Rucon, or his son, Ian. He wondered if that were possible.

The four-armed being stopped in the center of the room and spun slowly, taking in the others. He appeared to be as out of place as Armond, and ambled over to sit two rows below. It cast a furtive glance at Armond with bulbous round black eyes, before returning its attention to the rest of the assembly.

The ambient energy built as more occupants arrived. He'd caught glances from virtually everyone.

A silvery-skinned creature entered the room next. After a quick scan, it climbed up and sat a short distance from him.

"Greetings. I'm Anak-Sidar."

Again, the lips didn't align with those of a Common Language speaker. Nestled in a recess on the side of the creature's head was a device similar to his own. On the outside was the same symbol he'd seen on the shirts in the hall. So, probably the logo of the contest, then.

"I am Armond Nolde."

Anak made no gesture for physical contact such as a hand shake.

Armond leaned a little closer. "Are you familiar with this contest?"

"We are not. However participation appears to be the only way to return to our ship. Is this the way for you?"

"Yes." Sign the forms or don't go home.

No one had entered the room for over ten minutes, and a quick head count gave him forty-two participants. That made twenty-one teams. The sapphire woman across the room had an entire group entertained with whatever she was going on about. Gods be kind and don't put her with him.

Multi-colored lights flicked on and off, and music emanated from somewhere overhead.

The doors slid open a moment later, and twenty-one people filed in, including Candi. She waved at him and blew an air-kiss. He wondered what exactly being a handler to the contestants meant. Hopefully not too much time together. He'd play the damn fool game and return to Earth as soon as possible. He would also determine a way in which to come back here at his leisure. An entirely new galaxy to explore was extraordinary. As long as it was on his terms.

Following the handlers, three others entered the room. There was a white-haired man and two younger women, both with blonde hair and rather attractive. The male wore an obnoxious silver-sequined suit with metallic silver shoes, the women skimpy shorts with tight tee-shirts. The logo was large and centered on the front. "The Great Space Race. Octiron Corp."

What kind of race, he wondered. In the air above the three were a half dozen small flying orbs. They spanned out around the room. A number zeroed in on him, and spent nearly a minute inspecting him before zooming off, only to be replaced by others. They each had unique identifying marks, and he guessed they were video feeds.

A public contest then. It made sense. One came within inches of his face, and he resisted the urge to flick it away.

From the center of the room, a column rose, seamlessly forming into a podium. Perhaps it was similar to the technology employed in the training arenas on Sandaria. That required a tremendous amount of energy, and wasn't a sustainable substance. When the power died, so did the elements created. So many things to explore.

The man stepped up to the podium, flanked by the

women. They were a good foot taller than him, and at least twenty years his junior. "Welcome one and all! I want to thank you for coming here today. My name is Suede Harrington, which I'm sure our local participants already know." He preened and, judging by the doe-eyed women in the crowd, he had good reason to.

"We are very excited about the new contest! Take a moment to wave to the media's vidbots." Suede raised his arms and the devices whirled around the room. "This season is going to be extraordinary, and filled with surprising and exciting challenges. So, without further delay, let's get our contestants paired!"

"Attention!" The blonde to his right clapped her hands. "Handlers, please go and stand with your contestant on the left side of the room. All others who have yet to be assigned a handler, please gather on the right."

The room soon divided into two groups, with Candi standing next to him.

The dark-skinned woman was literally bouncing up and down on the other side. Her energy was clearly infectious, as the people next to her were also highly animated. Their exuberance was disconcerting, for he rarely found himself among such a group.

Harrington then proceeded to have the blondes distribute small coins to each of the contestants. Those with handlers had blue and those without, red. His had the image of a six-legged animal with a barbed tail.

"Does everyone have their coins?" Harrington asked.

"Don't you know it!" The sapphire-skinned woman's voice reverberated through the room. Unlike Candi, hers was low and smoky-sounding.

"All right then. Find your matches!"

"Come on," Candi said walking to the center.

Armond held his coin face out, and felt like a fool.

They'd barely begun the process when a sound to their left had all heads turning.

The gods were surely laughing at him. The sapphire woman held up the matching red coin, her face alight with a beaming smile. "I noticed you when you came in. You're very tall aren't you? Are you from here? Fan of the contest?"

"Hello, darling." Candi pushed her way between them. "I'll be your handler. I take it you're a fan of the show?"

"Oh yes. I never miss an episode. I can't believe I was selected. I was just between jobs and kind of drifting, you know, and figured what the heck, right? So I applied, and I can tell you, when I got the notice, I was stunned into silence."

Now that was something he'd like to see. At least he knew this wasn't the woman referenced by Marco and Zara. There was no compatibility here.

"What's your name, sweetheart?" Candi asked.

"I'm Vin Karatinatoochi." She bounced on her heels.

"That's a mouthful," Candi said.

"We'll stick with Vin. And who's my new partner?" Her eyes were so brown they were nearly black, and they were alive with vitality.

"This is Armond. He's from another galaxy, and thrilled to be here." Candi raised one eyebrow at him.

The three stood there for a long moment. Neither of them had asked a direct question, so he remained silent.

The vidbots swarmed around them.

"Well," Vin said, grasping her hands together. "Nice to meet you."

"Has everyone found their partners?" Harrington called out.

Shouts went up around the room, including from Vin. She was, in fact, the loudest.

Vin had a number of excess pounds on her, and he

wondered how that would affect their ability to compete. Of course, there was no indication that the competition had any physical component to it. But she may be a handicap, and her level of intelligence was unknown. He'd have to watch her closely, and compensate for any deficiencies.

"Are we going to be informed of the parameters of the competition any time soon?"

"All in good time," Candi said. "First, we must attend the opening gala so the press can meet everyone."

Vin clapped her hands in small precise movements. "I've watched every one. It's Chef Paul, He works magic with the dishes."

Armond had no response to that.

Vin crossed her arms and tilted her head. "You're an odd one, aren't you?"

He certainly wasn't the odd one in this gathering. "Can you at least inform me of the duration of the contest?"

Candi started to respond, but Vin beat her to it. "You never know. It all depends on how long it takes everyone to complete their tasks. Or fail them. But even then, there can be upsets when the judges get through with the scoring."

Nowhere in that response was there a timeframe. He tried to keep his tone of voice level. "Can you give me minimum and maximum estimates?"

"A few years ago, they finished in twelve days," Vin said.

Armond wondered how many hours were in a standard day in this region.

"Yes," Candi jumped in. "But that was highly unusual."

"True," Vin said. "Three seasons ago, the contest lasted nearly five months."

He couldn't imagine spending five months with anyone, this woman in particular.

"All right then," Harrington called out. "Everyone, please

go with your handler, and we'll see you tonight. I expect you all to be bright and shiny!"

Shouts of Bright and Shiny erupted from the crowd.

"Come along," Candi said. "We don't want to be stuck with the leftovers for gala attire. And you two are going to be difficult to dress, what with your height and your...size." She said the last to Vin directly.

Vin's smile appeared genuine, even though it was a slight at her size. Her white teeth were a stark contrast to her deep blue skin. "I'm sure I'll manage. Not so sure about Armond here."

"Indeed," Candi said. "Custom tailoring for you."

Vin made a deep sound of agreement. "Can I shop while he gets measured? I already know which stores I want to hit. I've drooled over their clothes for years."

"That would be acceptable. We need to retrieve your contestant packets first. They will have your credit discs."

Vin made another stereophonic sound. "I forgot about that. Let's go find out how much we have. I swear, I'll spend my own credits if it has a zero balance."

Candi frowned at Vin. "You know that's against the rules."

"Are you going to tell me that Sharla from last season was able to get that snazzy red number with only five credits? Everyone knows she found a way to pay for that herself."

Candi laughed. "In my official capacity as a handler, I have nothing to say regarding how Sharla may or may not have procured said garment."

"Ha! I knew it." Vin virtually skipped along beside them as they wove their way through the crowd and out the door. For a large woman, she was surprisingly spry on her feet.

Two hours later, Armond stood in front of a mirror, appalled. He was used to wearing the Earth Protector attire of black jeans and button up shirt. Black was a good color. It was acceptable for every occasion. He only owned a handful of items that were not black, and the purple and green monstrosity they had him in now was ludicrous. And stripes, no less. The only upside was that the other contestants' attire was equally preposterous, the men in particular. One wore a suit of green with multi-colored ornaments woven into the fabric.

The atmosphere in the store was becoming party-like as they approached the time for the event, and parties were not his forte. All he wanted to do was get this over with. If he ever made it back home, he would never speak of this to anyone.

Candi finally returned, with Vin in tow. Once again, the handler was dressed in fuchsia, with a neckline that nearly reached her navel.

Vin wore a cerulean blue dress that sparkled when she moved. It hugged her ample curves, and was seductively appealing. Her shoes were strappy numbers, and he had no idea how she managed to walk in those heels. Apparently some things were universal.

"Wow," Vin said, taking in his appearance. "You're very... colorful." Her eyes danced with humor.

After a pregnant pause, Vin spun. "What do you think?"

"You look...acceptable." Armond didn't do compliments.

Vin ignored his response and twirled again, watching herself in the floor-length mirror. There was no mistaking the woman's confidence.

"All right, my darlings," Candi said. "We have your inter-view sessions starting in twenty minutes. Dinner isn't until eight. Anyone need something to hold them over?"

"Anything in the offing from Chef Paul?"

"Why, of course there is." Candi eyed Vin from top to bottom. "Come with me. You won't be disappointed. Just remember to save room for later." She led them to a large room with bar-height tables scattered throughout. Along the back wall was a buffet that ran for thirty feet.

"Oh my nebula, would you look at that?" Vin made her way to the head of the table. "So much food, so little time!"

She had two plates laden with succulent meats and seafood within minutes.

Candi watched her returning to the table. "Do you think she'll be able to eat all that?"

He thought it doubtful but, true to her word, she sampled everything. That explained her curves.

Unsure of the compatibility of the food with his physiology, he selected one small processed item that looked like bread, and another small berry. Best to start slow.

"You'll like those," Candi pointed to the dark fruit on his plate. "They're pixberries. Delicious."

She assured him everything was safe, but for all he knew, the contest had already begun and poisoning was an option.

He placed the berry in his mouth. She wasn't wrong. It was sweet and succulent, with a tinge of sour in the aftertaste.

"Oh my," Vin said a few minutes later. "I think I've died and carried over. There isn't a single thing here that I didn't like." She'd eaten a rather extraordinary amount of food. Probably more than he'd be able to consume in one sitting. It reminded him of the Earth tradition of overeating on a holiday known as Thanksgiving, although she showed none of the usual signs of discomfort. If anything, she was even more energized than before. Perhaps she had a high-functioning metabolism.

There was a stark intelligence in her gaze. One that could be easily overlooked and underestimated, but perhaps that was by design.

Time would tell and he'd be watching.

CHAPTER 2

*T*hree hours later Armond stood around a small cocktail table next to Vin and Candi. It had been an endless stream of media-hyped nonsense.

Vin talked a great deal, but when she asked questions, they were very well thought out from the perspective of gathering intelligence, drawn out in such a way that it wasn't obvious. During the evening, she'd shifted her approach and communication style according to whom she was talking.

It suggested that her carefree appearance belied a keen intellect. He hoped so.

They'd made their way around the room and chatted with every other team. He'd been taking copious mental notes on each, trying to find any strengths or weaknesses that might be useful.

"So then, I was thinking this must be a joke, you know? Like someone had a vid feed on me and was waiting to jump out and laugh. But it didn't happen, and then I got the official confirmation for contest entry and I nearly passed out." Vin was speaking to the cat woman, Sarr'ma.

"I'm Tripp Gallifer." Her partner turned his attention to Armond.

"Armond Nolde."

"You in this willingly?" The burly man had a weather-worn face and brown eyes.

"Willing is a subjective term here."

He let out a guffaw and nodded agreement. "You got that right, partner. Looks like you have a chatty one on your hands."

Vin hadn't let up, but Sarr'ma didn't appear to mind.

"So, what do you figure we're going to have to do?"

"I have no idea." A subtle probing told Armond that Tripp had no psi. "Are you from this galaxy?"

"No, sir. We got ourselves intercepted during a portal. It was one hell of a long trip, I can tell you that. Thought we were dead."

"I experienced similar phenomena. The potential distance that could be traveled with a port of that duration is most impressive."

"Ya got that right. Scared me half to death."

Armond nodded as the bell rang, signaling it was time to move to the next contestants.

They made it through the rest of the evening without incident. Vin ate and talked, continuing with questions that turned up a great deal of information.

The event finished up with a dessert bar featuring dozens of delicacies, many of which he'd never seen the likes of. Particularly intriguing were the small figurines that radiated light and appeared to be alive. Unable to stem his curiosity, he selected one from the passing server and placed it on his palm.

Vin did the same, selecting three different varieties.

He held the tripodal creature up to the light.

"Aren't they amazing? And delicious too." Vin popped one

into her mouth. It was a provocative move, and left a trace of glowing powder on her plump lips.

He analyzed the thing with his psi, and found no living matter. "How is it able to move?"

"You could ask Chef Paul, but he won't tell you his secrets. It's one of his hallmark items. He once made a twenty-eight-foot serpentine creature that slithered all along the banquet table. Even after everyone dug in, all the little segments kept moving till the very end."

He eyed the animated confection dubiously. For all he knew, it was radioactive. Until he could get access to the proper equipment to run chemical analysis on food, he would consume with caution.

"You going to eat that?" Vin asked, eyeing the confection.

"Do you always eat this much?"

"Only when the food is this outstanding." She raised one eyebrow, and he held out his palm to her.

She placed her hand alongside his, her skin smooth and warm, and the thing walked across.

He couldn't take his eyes off her mouth as she held it open and let the delicacy waltz inside.

Her full lips once again dusted with glowing powder, she maintained a sexy smirk as she licked them clean. Everything she did had a sensual tint to it.

Candi appeared at their sides a moment later, disapproval of Vin's propensity for consumption written on her face. "Well, are you two ready to see your new home for the duration of the competition?"

"Will we be remaining on this planet, then?" Armond asked.

She let out her annoying laugh before answering, "That wouldn't be much fun, now would it?"

"We get a spaceship!" Vin playfully stroked his arm.

Unaccustomed to contact, he stifled the instinct to flinch.

"Haven't you seen the show before?" Vin asked.

"Never heard of it before today."

Her touch lingered as her expression sobered. "That's a major disadvantage. Can we get access to the previous seasons on the ship?" she asked Candi.

"Absolutely. You two need to win this thing for me."

"Watch it." Vin turned her attention back to him. "I mean it. You're a liability otherwise."

Her calling him a liability was laughable, so he simply nodded.

"Do you fly? I haven't flown anything larger than a two-seater. Last season there were a couple, and neither of them flew. The AI had to do it all for them. Messed it up more often than not."

Candi rolled her eyes.

"I am a highly trained pilot in an array of spacecraft," he assured them both.

Vin sported a lop-sided grin and did a little dance move. "And we have a pilot."

Candi led them from the room, stopping to say goodbye to individuals and media as they went.

They returned down the hall, past where they'd been assigned their partners, and into a glass elevator. Unlike those on Earth, this traversed not only vertically, but horizontally as well. The craft breached the exterior of the corporation and, for the first time, Armond saw the planet beyond.

A green-blue sky was dotted with dual moons and fast-moving clouds. Below, a great deal of vegetation interspersed with the cityscape beyond. A large river wound its way through structures that ran the gauntlet from single story to mega buildings like the one that housed what must be Octiron.

Once outside, they continued their ascent. By the time

they moved horizontally again, they had to be at least a hundred stories in the air. More impressive, some of the tree-like growth was nearly as tall. Stunningly thin reddish-brown trunks sprouted branches that spanned seemingly impossible distances. Armond wished he could get a better look, as some of them appeared to join together near the top of the canopy.

The room slowly rotated until they faced a fair-sized airfield. Dozens of spaceships of varying configurations dotted the tarmac. They skirted along the perimeter until coming to a stop behind a sleek number that looked like a high-end personal transport similar to that which the Cavacent Clan owned.

VIN KEPT HER FOCUS ON THE VIEWS BEYOND. THE PLANET WAS just as beautiful in person as it was on the broadcasts. She had to force herself not to stare at Armond. She'd never come across an individual so completely closed off. Zero emotion, he was a true enigma. Were all his people like this? Was she unable to access his emotions, or did he simply not possess any? She hoped it was the former. An entire race devoid of any kind of passion was a terrifying thought. She had a deep desire to find the answer.

One thing was perfectly clear: Candice had a chip on her shoulder a mile-wide where she was concerned. That was fine. She rubbed a lot of people the wrong way. Many were simply overwhelmed by her energy.

"It will be such fun watching you two." Candice stroked Armond's muscled arm, and continued to ignore Vin.

At least she knew how this was going to play out. The viewers would love the animosity between them. She should probably try to be more bitchy to increase ratings, but honestly, that just wasn't her style. Candice would just have to do her best to piss her off.

The transport came to a halt, and the door slid open. A crisp breeze whipped at her hair as they stepped out. The air was heavy with the scent of the flowering Windaria trees below. Damn things were beautiful, but they set off her allergies.

"This little baby here is yours," Candice said. They made their way across the tarmac to the ship's bow. She was long and sleek, a true beauty of a spacecraft. The name was imprinted just below the bridge viewscreen; *Galaxy Riders*.

Candice dug around in her ridiculously large purse and brought out two com units. She swiped across the screen of one and entered a code. A door appeared on the side of the hull and stairs slid out from underneath, coming to rest at their feet.

"Here you go." She handed Armond one of the units, then ascended the stairs.

"Guess I'll have to ask for my own," Vin said, shaking her head as a media vidbot zoomed past.

"So it would seem. After you," Armond stepped aside and let her go next.

As soon as she entered, it hit her, and she took a deep breath. "Nothing like that new-ship smell. How did we get so lucky?"

"There was a behind-the-scenes battle over who would supply our fleet. A new company won the contract."

More like stole is what Candi was thinking, Vin thought.

"Survive and it's yours. Everything is top-of-the-line, including a brand new AI system. It's designed to be more helpful than previously. I would suggest you make sure to leverage its knowledge as best you can."

"That should be interesting," Vin said. "They didn't do

anything before except navigation, and that they messed up half the time. It was hysterical."

"I don't see the humor in that," Armond said.

"Do you see the humor in anything?" Vin asked, giving him her most suggestive smile.

"Occasionally. When something is, in fact, humorous."

Was he teasing her? She studied his face. It was impossible to tell, which was as frustrating as a reluctant orgasm.

"Come along, the departing ceremony is in an hour. I'm sure you'll want to get changed into your travel clothes and get ready."

"I assume our clothes and toiletries are provided?" Armond asked.

"I keep forgetting you're new to all this," Vin said. "They provide everything, except for the stuff they don't. It's hysterical. Last time three contestants didn't have deodorant, one woman with hair thicker than mine didn't have a brush, another had no shampoo. And you can't borrow anything. You have to make do with what they give you. Isn't that a riot?"

Armond raised an eyebrow at her, which was the closest thing to emotion she'd seen so far. She decided it was a step in the right direction.

Candice gave them the tour, starting with the bridge. Top-of-the-line was an understatement. Even she could tell the equipment and console were impressive. She reached out, but felt absolutely nothing from the man next to her. Surly he would be pleased by this?

Candice, on the other hand, was a hot mess of desire where Armond was concerned. She pulled up her com and entered something. "Marty, I want you to meet Armond and Vin. They are your crew. Treat them accordingly."

"Greetings," a male voice surrounded them. "I am looking forward to working with you."

"Hello, I'm Vin." She waited for Armond.

He said nothing. She nudged him with her elbow. Or tried. He was a rock. "You need to say something so he can identify your voice."

A slight nod and Armond responded. "Greeting, ship's AI. I am Armond."

"Identification complete. And call me Marty. AI is so impersonal."

Next, Candi took them to the galley. It had a nice-sized kitchen and lounge area.

"Wow." Along the far wall was a viewscreen that ran the length of the room.

"Far more than wow." Candice dripped sarcasm. She toyed with the com unit and the screen turned opaque, displaying the tarmac outside. Another key sequence, and the surface morphed into a massive stone fireplace. The flames were at least five feet high, and a delicious warmth spread across her face.

"Oh, my. Just what you need in the cold of space." She rubbed her hands together and stepped closer. It was brilliant.

"The kitchen is fully automated or, if you wish, you can use the provided cookware and do it yourself." Candice looked like an oversized version of the creamed chocolate truffle Vin had eaten for dessert. In an unappetizing kind of way.

"Do you cook, Armond?" Candice was back to stroking Armond's bicep. "A big man such as yourself must eat a lot. Rather like our Vin here."

She was not *her* Vin. Less so by the second. She liked food, that wasn't a crime. And yes, there was a chance she'd out-eat the man. She could eat virtually anything and never gain weight. Didn't lose any either, and she was good with that.

Candice took them to the sleeping quarters next. Armond's first, of course. It was a decent size with a large bed in the center. "Our seamstresses have been working overtime to provide you with clothing," she told Armond. "I had them make clothes similar to what you arrived in. I thought you'd be more comfortable that way."

"You were correct," Armond said.

And there it was. The faintest hint of emotion when he replied, but it was gone in an instant. It was emotion, though, she was sure of it. Okay, so Iceman wasn't all ice after all. She'd find out what was buried under that cold exterior.

"Go check the bathroom," Vin said. "Make sure you have soap and all that."

He left for the small room off the side and returned a moment later. "It appears the only thing I'm lacking is a hair brush."

Oh dear. All that long blond hair and no brush? She wondered if he'd let her braid it for him. She liked the idea of running her fingers through his mane. Liked it a lot, in fact.

Candice took them to Vin's quarters next.

"Seriously?" Vin walked over and stood in the spot where there should have been a bed.

Candice radiated smug satisfaction. She'd known one of them would go without, and had purposefully assigned Vin. Oh well, there were worse things to be missing. She was relived to discover she had ample soap, shampoo, and tooth-paste, and even some makeup.

They wrapped up the tour in the engine compartment and cargo bay. Five numbered lockers lined one wall.

Armond seemed to know a lot about the technical aspects of the ship, and given her computer skills, they were a solid team. She mentally reviewed all the information she'd gleaned from the other contestants during the banquet, and decided their chances were pretty damn decent.

Candice finished the tour back at the entry. Two large wheeled crates sat by the inner door. "These are your clothes for the duration," Candice said. "Wear whatever you plan to fly in. Adds flavor for the viewers. I'll be back in an hour to escort you to the departure ceremony. It's right outside on the tarmac, in the center of all the contestants' ships. The crews are busy setting up the function now."

"Remember that time the ships were cleared for launch before they finished cleaning up the space? That was spectacular! Servers went flying everywhere!" It was one of her favorite episodes. The amount of food that had been wasted in the carnage still made her weep.

A look of worry crossed Candice's face. "Yes. Let's hope the producers aren't planning a repeat of that stunt. It wasn't only the servers who went flying that evening."

Feelings of anger and betrayal enveloped the handler. It surprised Vin. She'd always assumed that the handlers were in on everything.

"I'll see you!" Candice's sing-song voice grated more each time she spoke.

The outer door slid shut, and she turned to Armond. "She has *such* an annoying voice."

"Agreed."

"Okay, then, Mr. Chatty. Time to get dressed," Vin said. "Help me get this to my room?"

He took both crates without a word.

She watched him walk away. She wasn't picking up on his emotions, but there was something else happening. Something new. Different. It felt like a vibration more than an emotion, but it definitely originated from Armond. This day just got more and more intriguing.

Twenty minutes later, Vin was showered and had gone through the contents of her clothing crate. Two things were missing. One was something to sleep in, and the other was underwear. Plenty of bras, thank the gods. Her girls were too big to go free-range all day. She had a lot of shirts too, but they were too short to cover her ass. Without underwear, it left her sleeping in pants, which wasn't going to happen. Still, it could have been worse. "Let the games begin."

~

VIN FINISHED PUTTING ON SOME MAKEUP AND TAMING HER hair before locating Armond in the galley. The vid screen bustled with servers and crew out on the tarmac, setting up tables and getting ready for the event.

Armond's dark pants were form fitting and showed off a seriously nice tush. His buttoned-up shirt accentuated his muscular physique. Black synth boots completed the drool-worthy ensemble. His long white hair was in a neat ponytail at the nape of his neck. Yeah, she wanted to run her hands through it all right.

The tarmac had been transformed into a stunning sight. High-top tables stood in front of a stage large enough to hold all the contestants. It was standard for the launch ceremony to have them all together for the sendoff. She'd have to see what further information she could get from the others. They'd run into individual teams, but not all of them, and probably not more than a few at a time. That's the way it worked.

"It's beautiful," she said standing next to Armond.

He looked at her with eyes that had only a hint of blue, and knew that he was pondering the word beautiful.

"Don't you think?" she prompted.

"Beauty is a subjective concept."

"True, but many things are somewhat universal if you have a similar enough humanoid background. Like that scene out there. That's very pretty."

"If you say so."

Not much of a conversationalist this one, but he had hidden depths, of that she was certain. "So, anything missing from your clothes?" He appeared fully equipped.

"I am lacking in underwear."

She couldn't stop the laugh. "You too? That's so funny. How about pajamas? Do you have those?"

"I don't require them."

The image that came along with the words was pure decadence. "But did you get some?"

He looked down at her. The man was tall. "I did."

"Like a soft shirt?" His would at least come to her knees.

"Two."

"Can I have them? They gave me nothing to sleep in, and no undies either. Please?"

"I thought that was against the rules."

"They aren't filming yet. At least, they're not supposed to be. If we get them now, no one will know."

"Until you go to bed in my shirts."

"They don't film the bedrooms unless you allow it." They weren't supposed to, at any rate. "Please? Before Candi comes back?"

As usual, there were no emotional cues or facial expressions as he looked at her. "All right."

His acquiescence surprised her. Probably because she simply had no baseline to draw from. She followed to his room and grabbed the shirts, then sprinted back and shoved them in her crate.

They'd just returned to the galley when Candice appeared at the doorway. She now wore a silvery metallic dress that would reflect every color out there. "Well, don't you two look lovely." Her eyes never left Armond.

"Thanks. I love these flowing pants and tight top," Vin said. No doubt Candice had played a role in their selection.

She probably assumed Vin wouldn't like the way they hugged her ass, but that was one of her finest features.

"Shall we proceed to the tarmac? The press is anxious for final farewells." Candice definitely wasn't pleased.

The sun was setting as they emerged from the ship. The air was crisp, but not cold. A hint of a breeze carried the sticky scent of windaria.

The event area was stunning. The way the multi-colored globes floated over the gathering left the tarmac looking like someone had spilled paint over everything and everyone. High-top tables were scattered throughout.

Vin leaned closer to Armond and pointed to the stage. "That's where we'll get our first task. After that, we'll be working for them."

A barely perceptible nod was his only response.

They made their way across the gathering. It took a long time, with media peppering them with questions every few feet.

On stage, Suede Harrington set down a briefcase and stood back. A moment later, a translucent multicolored podium rose from the case. It was an enchanting kaleidoscope of colors, mirroring those present in the air above.

Music picked up with a lively beat.

The ships were all stunning; glistening things of beauty. There was a tension in the air and the energy was thick with a wide range of emotions. This was it. They couldn't turn back if they wanted to. Vin had always known this may be a one-way trip. If that was the case, she was going to enjoy every last second. Starting with the long table of sweets set up in the rear. She left Armond and Candi, and headed over.

She'd just devoured her third animated delicacy when Mac Wendorn strolled over, followed by four vidbots that settled into a hover a few feet above them.

"Vin Karatin...Karatintoo... Darlin', you have a last name

that was never meant to be broadcast." He reached out and plucked an eight-legged confection off the platter and plopped it into his mouth. "Are you ready?" he said around the treat.

"Absolutely," she said. "I clearly have an advantage." She motioned to Armond, who watched her from his position next to Candi. She held that gaze. What was hidden behind those nearly colorless eyes? She licked her fingers slowly, provocatively. From this distance, it was hard to tell, but she'd swear he was watching her lips. They weren't her worst quality. The thought of this cold, indifferent being harboring a passionate side stirred something deep within. What would it be like to have those arms of steel exploring her body? Would he be interested in a woman like her? Hells, for all she knew, he could prefer men, or be asexual.

And still he stared.

She took longer than necessary to clean the sugar from her fingers, and finished by licking her lips. His gaze lingered a moment before looking away.

"Ain't that right?" Mac said.

"Sorry, what?"

"I said, he may be powerful-looking, but we don't know what he's made of, now do we? Not even from our galaxy. Could be fragile as a flame."

"True." He could be, but she didn't think so. The man radiated power.

The music hit a crescendo as Suede Harrington spoke up from the stage. "I need all contestants to come on up!"

"Looks like we're on," Vin said, snatching one last delight.

"We'll be seeing you soon, darlin'. And often." Mac was so ecstatic about the whole thing, it was almost creepy.

Vin tracked Armond's path and converged with him before the steps. The teams stood, randomly spaced behind the podium. The press gathered around.

The orbs above brightened and, as if on cue, a gust of wind whipped over the people, unseating more than a few hats. Squeals of laughter erupted as men and women chased them down.

Once everyone was settled again, a hush fell over the group.

Suede stood, chest puffed out like a prize fighter.

Vin doubted the man could walk a mile, let alone run one.

The women flanking him each held a jeweled box clutched to their ample chests. On a table behind them were the rest of the boxes, each a unique design.

Suede lifted his right hand, and the closest woman placed a box gently onto his open palm. Stroking the thing like a lover, he placed it on the podium. "Are we ready to begin?"

The crowd erupted in cheers and whoops. Their fellow contestants radiated a mix of emotions from elation to fear.

For her, it was something akin to resigned anticipation. One way or another, this was going to be an adventure.

"You all know the routine," Harrington's voice boomed across the space. "Once each contestant has read their objective aloud, they will return to their ships until I give the clear for departure signal." He really should stop fondling that damn box.

Within minutes, the first three contestants were off, each with a cryptic message and destination to be revealed after they left the exosphere.

They were fourth to get called to the podium. Vin wiped the sweat from her palms and stood next to Armond. A faint hint of something crisp and clean tickled her nose. She shifted her weight slightly and leaned in closer to the man. Trying not to be obvious, she inhaled deeply. She couldn't help a slight moan as his unique aroma settled over her.

Harrington continued his box fondling as he lifted the lid and handed her a small scroll from within, only four or five inches long, nodding to the mic for her to read it to the gathering.

She unfurled the parchment and cleared her throat.

"Our destination is a planet called Altaria, also known as Farewell. This is our clue:

Underground and out of place you'll have to squeeze into this space.

Retrieve the gem, but do not tarry, when they return it could get scary.

Beware the things upon the ground,

the ones you like can take you down."

Her stereophonic voice echoed through the night when she finished. The silence was oddly weighted. Heavy with destiny. Or something else.

She met Armond's gaze. "Let's go."

ONCE ON BOARD, THEY MADE SURE EVERYTHING WAS SECURE and ready for flight. They were itching to go, but had to wait for the rest of the contestants to receive their clues and finally for the press and tarmac to clear. It was a comical process once the last task had been read. No doubt the premature departure echoed through their memories, as waitstaff hurriedly cleared the deck, casting furtive glances at the ships powering up.

They settled into the bridge and strapped in. She leaned over the posh console and pulled up the first-rate nav system. It hadn't taken her any time to sort through the controls and figure out the interface.

"Do we have the coordinates yet, Marty?" Vin asked.

"I will supply that information as soon as it arrives." Marty had an air of superiority about him. "Assuming we make it that far."

"He's right," Vin said. "Watch it when we have the clear

signal. There's frequently some idiot disqualified before they even get off the planet."

The ships were arranged in a circle, which made for an obvious departure pattern. Up and outward, but someone always mangled it.

"It is a dangerous way to begin," Armond said.

"Not as much as it appears. They have tractor beams to protect the building. It's just a lousy way to lose."

"Once we're up and you have the coordinates, set our course immediately and jump as soon as possible. I'll catchup with my calculations." Vin sat back to watch the proceedings.

"There's no need to verify my destination." Marty said.

"No offense, but I'm not going to trust you, given the previous season's AIs."

"Fine. It's your wasted time cycles."

Vin grinned at the petulant response. "Time to get this party started." She checked the air traffic. "All local traffic patterns are on hold for our departure. It's an eight-mile diameter."

Suede Harrington's voice came over the com. "Tarmac is clear. Good luck, and may the best team win!"

"We don't need luck." Armond lifted off with practiced ease.

Sure enough, a sleek craft veered off at a bad angle, and forced another to jet out sideways. Something was wrong with the first ship, and it headed back down.

"Wonder if that's operator error or mechanical failure?" Vin said.

With a confidence that only came with experience, Armond located a clear path and they rocketed skyward.

Three minutes after leaving the planet's atmosphere, Marty provided the coordinates to Altaria. Once she had it, Vin brought up all known information on their destination. As expected, the intel was sparse, to keep them guessing.

She scanned the data before re-reading the clue. Pulling up the holo projection, she zeroed in on an area in the south east of the southern hemisphere. "According to this, there's a large network of subterranean caves here." She pointed to the lush green region. "And this appears to be to most likely entrance."

"Given our lack of more detailed information, that sounds reasonable."

As usual, his emotional energies were a void. He was a true enigma. Although he must be shielding his emotions, she could detect no such indicator. And she always found them. She'd never met a sentient being who could truly hide from her, until now. The only crack in his shell, when Candi mentioned his clothing. Or perhaps she'd imagined that?

Vin bit back a smile. It was a challenge. And more than a little bit of a turn-on. It looked like there was more than one game in play, and she liked winning.

CHAPTER 3

"*A*ren't you the least bit curious about the rest of the planet?" A day and a half, and Vin had yet to elicit any emotional frequency from Armond. And she'd come at it from every angle she could think of.

The surface of Altaria filled the viewscreen of the bridge, growing larger as they descended.

"I am, of course, curious, but we have a task to complete and a contest to win."

Vin sat next to Armond as he eased the ship down with a feather-light touch on a grassy area not far from where she'd located the cave entrance.

Lush green and orange vegetation filled the dense forest outside. A riot of flowers covered the place in nearly neon colors. Wisps of clouds trailed across the blue sky above.

Armond shut down the engines, and they peeled themselves out of the cush command chairs.

"You weren't kidding when you said you knew how to fly." She stretched out her back.

"I've been flying since the age of twelve."

That was impressive by any standard. "Did your folks fly?"

"That is unknown."

Interesting. And how does that illicit zero emotion?

She did a scan of the atmosphere outside the ship. "Readings are all nominal. It's really humid, but beautiful."

"You use that word frequently." As always, Armond's posture was military perfect.

"I find beauty in many places."

"Its appearance doesn't mean it is any less dangerous."

"Or deadly. Duh. Did you watch any of the previous seasons like I suggested?"

"I have not had the time."

She gave him a scowl. "Liability."

He met her gaze, nothing more.

Born this cold, or made by circumstance? Strikingly handsome, he had one of those faces that made it impossible to tell his age. Could be thirty, could be sixty. Hell, with today's tech he could be over a hundred.

"Marty," she addressed the ship's AI, "anything we should know about this world? Dangers, in particular?"

"There are numerous venomous species on this planet, but there are no aggressive forms in the immediate area." The AI's voice was oddly modulated.

"Excellent." Vin activated Marty's remote interface on her com. "Shall we go?"

Armond gave her a curt nod. "I suggest we take advantage of the weapons they provided. I assume you know how to handle them?"

"Honey, I grew up on my uncle's farm on Trianth. Killing the small predatory animals before they ate our livestock was a full-time job."

The weapons locker was off the main entry to the ship.

She strapped on a laser, and secured a high-tech breathing apparatus around her neck.

Armond held another in his hand. "I am unfamiliar with this. What does it do?"

"Fully loaded, it can provide a couple hours of air. Watch." Vin activated the collar, and it snicked into place, enveloping her head one horizontal section at a time. Once fully deployed, she wore a snug-fitting helmet with decent visibility.

Armond tried to activate his without putting it on. Of course, nothing happened.

"You have to wear it." Vin pocketed a light and handed one to Armond.

He took it with a curt nod and he fastened the collar around his neck. But didn't try it out.

As if cued by an off-stage director, the reality of it all settled over her once again. She'd known exactly what this was, and the potential for danger, but somehow even signing the contract with all that language about dismemberment and stuff hadn't seemed real.

People died in this thing. It was also massively lucrative for survivors. And they'd get to keep this beauty of a ship. Or not. They'd probably have to sell it and divide the credits. Bummer, that.

They lowered the external stairs and walked into a balmy summer's afternoon. The damp clung to her skin. She'd pulled her hair into a tight tail, but the humidity would have her looking like a Trinathian bush cat in no time. Wiping her hand across her brow, it came away wet. "We're going to be soaked by the time we get out of here," she said.

"We're going to be soaked before we begin." It was an uncharacteristically long reply for the albino. Progress, maybe?

Their leather boots were nearly silent as they crossed the

lush green grassy area. She bent down to get a closer look at the growth. It was blue tinged, fine strands, and resembled hair more than anything.

Hovering overhead was an Octiron Vidbot. That sucker would probably stick with them like glue now.

"Say hello to our fans." Vin smiled and waved enthusiastically.

Armond did nothing. That was ok. There were always contestants that people loved to hate. He may fall into that category.

A refreshing breeze darted in from the south, and the entire field ruffled in waves. At the same time a tangy odor reached her. Tangy, with a hint of rot. "You smell that?"

"Yes. I'd guess organic."

"Possibly decomposing, which could draw scavengers." The intensity of the smell increased as the breeze picked up. "I bet that Yeealla couple is loving this if they're here now."

"Which couple?"

"The really thin ones, remember? You talked with them before the main course at dinner."

"You were occupied with Tygean Jag during that conversation."

She grinned. It always took people a while to figure her out, if they ever did. "I heard, all right. They have a highly developed sense of smell. Something about their genetic relation to the Yeeallas, who's primary sense is olfactory. That's a weird way to experience life, huh?" And there it was again. A hint, a whiff, a mere suggestion of surprise, or was it something else? Was he impressed?

Passing under moss-laden trees, they made their way to the cave entrance.

The moment they stepped inside, the temperature dropped a good fifteen degrees, sending goosebumps down her damp skin.

The entrance veered to the right and a faint glow emanated from around the bend. "Only one way to go. Marty, any life forms in here?" Her com emitted a staticky noise. "Marty?"

There was no further reply, so they made their way in silence. Whatever the light source was, it shone a lovely blue color, and illuminated the walls at the far end.

She reached out with her senses, and didn't find anything other than some insect-sized critters. Nothing sentient.

Armond had his laser in hand as they turned the corner.

"Nice." She stepped closer. "Crystalline. I wonder what the light source is."

"That's a question for another time. We have a mission to complete." He had to be ex-military.

She caught up to him and they continued deeper into the mountain. They'd been going down since entering the tunnel. Had to be below ground by now. Vin jumped when Marty's voice boomed from her com. "There appears to be a large number of..."

Silence followed. She checked the volume, but it was set on low, even though that voice had damn near blown out an eardrum.

"A large number of what, Marty?" she asked.

No answer.

"Are you picking up on anything?" she asked Armond.

"Nothing unusual."

"I wish we had a better idea of exactly what we're looking for. 'Underground and out of place you'll have to squeeze into this space.' Well, we haven't squeezed anywhere yet."

They'd been going for nearly thirty minutes when they came to a dead end. The light in the rocks had steadily increased, and it was quite luminous now, with an eerie blue hue. Like a clear night and a full blue moon.

"What do we do now?" Vin asked.

"My sensors indicate a large cavern directly ahead."

Vin reached out and touched the surface of the wall in front of her. "It's warm. Can you tell how thick it is?"

"The material is oddly refractive. I get different readings every time."

"Try blasting it?"

"That could bring the ceiling down on us."

She backed up a few feet and scanned the edges of the block. Along the right side, rock protruded up to the ceiling, forming something of a natural staircase. "There." She pointed to the place where the wall met the roof.

About two feet from the top, there was a slight shift in the light hue. "I think that's an opening."

She pocketed her com and started climbing. Usually, a male would caution her to be careful. Basic human nature stuff. But her albino remained silent. She wasn't sure how that made her feel. Was he trusting in her abilities, or simply not concerned? She'd go with the former, because why not?

The climb was easy, but it was twenty feet or so from the cave floor. She pressed her right shoulder against the wall and didn't look down. As she neared the top, there was indeed a ledge, and the light was brighter beyond. Deep within the walls, or possibly on the other side something moved. Or somethings. It was hard to say, as the shadows scattered in different directions, the light doing weird things in here. She approached the ledge and peered over. "We'll have to crawl through this. Probably means we're on the right track. Come on."

Whatever had moved was out of sight, so she pulled her laser from the holster and lay on her stomach to slither across the opening.

It was only five or six feet, and beyond was a massive subterranean cavern.

"God's Balls, come and see this."

43

Armond was behind her a moment later, moving freakishly fast. There was the slightest tinge of an emotional response as he bolted over the edge.

"Careful," she said. "Something was moving in here when I approached the ledge."

He landed a few feet below, weapon drawn and sweeping.

Maybe his chivalry had kicked in. Whatever. The place was stunning. And deep. She wasn't sure she could make out the end. Along the bottom, giant crystals jetted out at crazy angles. She'd never seen any so large. They glowed with the blue light from within. Some appeared to be ten or twelve stories high, with a circumference the size of her grandfather's house.

Armond started to make his way down to the cavern floor.

"It's beautiful, isn't it?"

He raised an eyebrow at her.

"Yeah, yeah, everything's beautiful, but just look at that, will you?"

Deep in the cavern, a massive shadow moved across a grouping of crystals. "You see that?"

"Yes."

The form moved to the left, then slid down to the ground and dissipated. There was nothing solid to be seen, just vague shapes behind the crystals.

"Keep your laser ready at all times," Armond said.

"Of course. I think I saw that same thing as I breached the surface of the ledge. More than one. Maybe." The descent was far more gradual. She was riding an adrenalin high as she followed Armond down. Who knew imminent danger could be so invigorating?

Somewhere in the distance, water, or liquid of some kind, dripped in a steady stream.

"What do you think?" Vin said when she reached the

bottom. "This place is enormous. Where do we start? We should split up, right?"

"In a potentially hostile environment, that would be unwise."

Vin got the impression he was taking in every single detail. Probably best to take his advice. "Straight back, then?"

"Agreed."

It was intimidating as hell to approach the crystals. Some were at acute angles, and she didn't like the thought of walking underneath them. More than one previously fallen soldier littered the floor. They rather looked like a rag tag army, guarding this place. "Can you tell how far back this goes? I can't see where the end is."

"It's the optics. I am unable to get an instrumental reading on it either."

Ahead, something changed. A shift in the acoustics. She couldn't figure it out at first, but it resolved quickly. Something was coming. And it was big.

Vin grabbed Armond's arm to stop him, and a blinding flash of a million emotions tore through her. She whipped up her empathic blocks and yanked her hand away, stunned by the sheer force of it. She blinked repeatedly, but her vision was blocked by the sensory overload. "We need to get under cover. And I can't see." This wasn't the first time it had happened, but it was the most severe. The man's cold, emotionless, exterior was cracked.

"Are you injured?" Armond asked.

"Not really. Just guide me." Whatever it was, it was coming fast. "What is it?"

"Unable to determine yet." The warmth of his touch seeped into her upper arm and her lower back as he hurried them off to the side. His emotions once again completely absent. He took her hand and placed it on a crystal. The thing leaned over them at a disturbing angle. "Kneel down," he said in a low voice.

She did as he said, pressing her back to the surface and sitting as close to the base as possible. The heat of his body pressed against her side and they waited.

"What happened to you?" His breath was hot on her neck as he whispered the question.

"I'll explain it later." Her sight was returning, but it was blurry as hell. She turned towards him. "What's happening?" His spicy scent enveloped her, and the image of kissing those lips flashed into her mind.

He tilted his face and pressed his lips against her ear. "Avian creatures of some kind."

The heat of his breath sent a shiver through her as her vision returned.

Armond reached up and activated her helmet before doing the same with his own.

The sound was a roar in the helmet's speakers and the entire cavern was filled.

"What are they?" Vin spoke low.

Armond's voice came across clear. "Small, black winged. I can't get a good look at their faces."

The creatures were streaming out the narrow ledge they'd crawled through, and many other openings along the periphery.

Too bad they weren't facing the other way, they might be able to determine the size of the place, or at least the source of the critters. On the upside, being under the crystal shielded them from the stuff falling from overhead. Mostly liquid, it pooled on the floor and sizzled before evaporating.

The flock was gone within minutes, and the final vestiges of the droppings dissipated as they watched. "Is that what I think it is?"

"If you think it's acidic, my guess is yes."

"Acid poop. Okay then."

They deactivated the helmets.

"Has your sight returned?" Beneath the spice of his breath was musk and wood. Masculine. Alluring.

"Yes."

"Are you certain you are well?"

His pale eyes held hers as another barely perceptible tinge of *something* emanated from him.

"I'm fine."

The crystal loomed overhead. Probably ready to snap and crush them like bugs. "Let's go. I don't want to be here when they return. Return! *When they return things could get scary.* Don't have to warn me. That shit's deadly." She laughed. "Literally."

"My assumption is they're feeding. It should be awhile."

"Yeah, well, I want to get out of here." She rolled to her right and stepped sideways out from under the crystal. "We kind of had to squeeze our way in here, so maybe we're almost done." The crystals sparkled as though just washed, which in a way, they had been.

As they continued deeper into the cavern, the ceiling became lower.

They walked until they entered another tunnel. Increasingly, bits of broken crystal and other rock-like formations littered the floor, forcing them to weave.

Armond scanned the area with his com in one hand, keeping his laser in the other.

"Are you getting anything useful?" Vin asked, stepping over a knee-high pillar.

"There is an anomaly ahead. Something that doesn't match the composition of the surroundings."

"Underground and out of place... Let's check it out."

As the ceiling continued to get lower, a resonance emanating from Armond became stronger. Totally devoid of recognizable emotion, but also clearly emotive of some kind. Was that what albino meant? Were all his people like this?

At the end of the tunnel, they found only one small opening. Vin knelt down and peered inside. The hole was probably twenty feet long, terminating in a room at the other end. And there, sitting in plain sight, lay a silver box bearing the GSR logo. It was surrounded by stunning pink crystals. "We got it." Almost. She surveyed the opening. "I'm not going to fit in there. You'll have to go and get it."

Armond knelt down next to her, and the resonance amped up a notch. When he extended his hand and closed his eyes, the resonance took on a different tone, one she found oddly enticing.

"What are you doing?" she asked.

"Trying to retrieve the box."

"With what?" Maybe her gorgeous albino had a screw loose.

"Psi, but it appears the crystals surrounding the box are either blocking or disrupting the energy."

"We're wasting time. Crawl in there and get it before it disappears. That's likely to happen if we delay. And you'd know that if you watched the previous seasons like I told you to."

The resonance coming off him was so high pitched it hurt. She shut down her receptors and eyed the large man. His body was motionless and tense as steel. "Are you claustrophobic?"

"Perhaps."

That would be a yes. "Sorry, but between my tits and my hips, I'm not going to fit. It's got to be you. I can help, though. I just make a psychic connection, and—"

"No." The response was immediate and absolute.

If that blinding breach earlier was any indication, he had

reason to keep his emotions in check. "I'm an empath. I can dampen your fear. Nothing else. Just your fear."

"You will attempt no such thing. Not now, not ever. Do you understand?"

"Fine, just get moving." Stubborn male.

He hit the ground and shot forward headlong in small, fast increments. It was tighter than she'd thought, but he kept going.

He was nearly midway when his body tensed and a barrage of fear blasted her. Short, staccato pulses, and he froze.

"Armond, you can do this. You have to relax." She spoke low and calm. He may not want her accessing his emotions, but she'd trained on Myranth and could modulate her voice to create a trance-like state. Then she could encompass his fear.

It wasn't ethical to do it without permission, and he had to listen for it to work, but she figured this was an emergency. She settled her energies and spoke a steady stream of encouragement. Within thirty-seconds, she shifted to a state of theta wavelengths and she had him. His fear was paralyzing, but he sensed her.

"Vin, stop."

"It's ok. You're all right. I have you. Do you feel that?"

A sense of wonder and astonishment pulsed over her before it was abruptly blocked. The last nanosecond had revealed a different kind of fear. Something vastly more complicated than that of a phobia.

Armond's body relaxed, providing a good inch of clearance, and he moved forward faster than before.

He reached the end and for a moment all she saw were his boots. He was back on the ground an instant later and moving at his freakish speed, clutching the box in one hand as he went.

Vin continued the semi-trance-like state until he was back with her and they were both standing.

He slowly handed her the box, his breathing elevated, but even. "What was that language?" he asked. "I've not heard it before."

"Not surprising. Very few people speak Myranthian." He didn't need to know it was a tool of advanced empaths who worshiped the divine light of creation. They were an interesting people, and it was a power that could be seriously abused in the wrong hands.

He studied her face with such intensity it had her fidgeting. "You are well?"

"Why do you keep asking me that?"

He shook his head. "Let's go."

They made their way back through the cavern and up to the ledge they'd entered. Vin was about to hoist herself up, but hesitated. "You think that acid poop is clear?"

Armond reached out and swiped his finger tip across the surface. "It would appear so."

Good enough. They went side by side this time, with Armond on the left. That meant he'd have to go first, as the only way down was the rocky bit in the corner.

"Give me the box while you go down. I'll toss it to you."

"I have a better idea." Whatever the hell that resonance thing he did was, it pinged full force. He handed her the box, swung his legs around, and stood on the nearest foothold. Without a word he reached in, took her by the arms, and pulled her out. They went over backward, and she instinctively flung herself around him as they fell. Only they didn't fall. A full-on body buzz erupted as they more or less floated to the ground. Gods, the man was rock solid.

He set her down, took the box, and started walking back to the cave entrance.

"What was that?" She rushed to catch up with him.

"That was psi. You have it as well. I can sense it."

"I don't know what psi is, and I assure you I can't fly."

"That wasn't flying. More like levitation, and that was close to my weight limit."

Was that an insult? It was hard to be angry, however, as her body still buzzed from the contact.

They exited the cave and headed for the ship. The smell had abated, and the blue sun was high in the sky.

High above the mountains, a dark cloud swarmed in a fluid dance. "Look." She pointed.

"They're feeding," Armond said.

"That means we made it!" She let out a whoop and twirled in celebratory circle.

Nearly there, Vin spied a brightly colored bed of flowers that extended from the base of a tall thin tree with delicate looking leaves. She pulled out her pocket laser and gathered a small handful, carefully slicing the stems in a clean sweep. The colorful stems jerked and tiny orbs opened in their faces. A hail of little blobs speckled her neck, hands, and lower arms.

She screamed and threw the flowers as her skin boiled where the substance had made contact. "Shit, they're alive."

Armond grabbed her hand and surveyed the damage. The skin bubbled and spat.

Pain shot from her neck and the left side of her face. The warmth of blood trickled down her collar. This was bad. Really bad.

Armond shook his head. *Beware the things upon the ground.*

The white of her bone became visible on her hand. Her head spun with the surreal sight. "We have to neutralize this. Marty, are you there?"

"I am present. Vin has been exposed to an acidic compound that will penetrate the carotid artery in her neck in approximately twenty-eight seconds."

"How do we stop it?" Vin asked.

"There is a compound on the ship that will work. I will have it waiting for you in the galley."

Armond scooped her up and ran. The stairs descended as they approached, and her body buzzed with that psi thing of his as they sailed through the air and into the entryway.

"Where is it?" Armond called out as they entered the galley.

"In the food replicator."

He laid her on the counter and retrieved the substance.

"We can't trust that," Vin said. The pain was intense, and yet she was somehow distanced from it. Probably in shock.

"You have no choice," Armond said. "You'll be dead shortly either way."

"Pour a small amount into each wound," Marty said.

He leaned over her and started to pour, when a spurt of blood shot out and into his face. A moment later, another stream jetted out.

This was it. Her artery had been penetrated. She was going to die over some stupid flowers.

CHAPTER 4

*A*rmond felt the moment Vin lost consciousness. He hadn't realized it, but her very presence had an essence. An energy that had been with him since they'd met. Standing over her now, the absence was unmistakable.

He ignored the copious amounts of blood and continued working. Using his psi, he staunched the flow from her artery long enough to apply the liquid. He waited a full fifteen seconds before allowing the flow to resume while simultaneously stitching the arterial wall together with psi. It was slow, and with multiple injuries he was burning a tremendous amount of energy. He applied the liquid to the other impact spots, and wiped away blood until he was sure he had them all.

He placed one hand near her neck and the other on her wrist, and closed his eyes. Reaching out, he evaluated the extent of damage to each site and went after them in order of necessity, all the while keeping the cellular stitching going on her artery. There weren't many in existence that could do this. The incident should have killed her.

Twenty-three minutes in, and his psi was approaching

depletion. He was in dangerous territory with his shields faltering, but he nearly had her stabilized. She would not die today.

The psi of an unconscious person was an untethered thing of beauty.

When he'd depleted his energy reserves to a nearly life-threatening amount, he pulled back. She was stable, for now.

And they were both covered in blood.

A small section of her shirt began to bubble and spit.

He whirled around and applied the neutralizer. Once done, he located a knife and removed her clothes as quickly as possible.

Her left boot also exhibited signs of the acid. Working rapidly, he dumped everything she'd been wearing into the incinerator.

Using a large sponge, he began cleaning her. Wipe, rinse, repeat. He had to ensure there were no spots left untreated. After completing an initial pass, he started over.

A sapphire body with curves unlike anything he'd experienced. Her skin was supple and soft where his fingers brushed against it. He gently lifted each breast and wiped underneath. Her beauty was undeniable.

Something had happened back in the cave. There had been a momentary flicker of his shields the moment she'd touched his arm.

When she'd said she couldn't see, he'd nearly panicked, but she was fine, and her sight had returned. Was it possible this woman could withstand the forces within him? Was she the one Marco Dar had mentioned?

His touch turned into a caress as he trailed his fingers across her arm.

A forbidden pleasure.

Stopping his movement, he openly stared at her. He

hadn't touched a woman since Dareena. Beautiful, young Dareena, only seventeen at the time...

Goosebumps rippled over her body. Armond gently picked her up and carried her to his room, placing her on the only bed in the ship. She would need sleep to heal, and he needed both sleep and food to restore his energy.

After eating enough to make Vin proud, Armond showered before pulling up a chair beside her. Within moments, he'd fallen into an exhausted sleep.

VIN FLOATED IN A SEA OF STARS. IT WAS LOVELY. WHICH heaven was this? Was her mother here? She wanted to see her again.

She focused on her...being. Tried to determine any sensory input. It felt as though she were lying down, which didn't seem right, but she felt good. Really, really good. A familiar kind of good. One she should recognize, but she couldn't put her finger on.

Heavy breathing echoed through the space. Near and far at the same time.

The pleasure was increasing. Tension furled in her center, building, before exploding into an orgasm that burst from her core. *That* kind of good. Of all the things she'd thought to experience when she died, that wasn't one of them. But then, why not?

The sensation rippled everywhere. She *was* the pleasure. She lost track of time, drifting in and out of awareness.

She existed as a point of light, zigging and zagging, creating ephemeral images. She danced with the universe.

Something tugged at her mind. Pulling her in. She was embodied, perched over a young girl. A beautiful girl with pale skin and wavy brown hair that splayed out across the pillow her head rested upon. Such joy and love written on her face. It changed in the space between heartbeats. Her eyes widened with fear and pain. Blood oozed from her nose, pooling beneath her ears. She shed tears of crimson.

A horrific sense of loss and power surged through her, defining her existence.

Someone cried out. Labored, irregular breathing echoed around her.

Vin.

She was with a group of robed men in a cave lit only by torches attached to the walls. They stood in a circle surrounding a stone obelisk that glowed red from within. The men appeared to be in some kind of trance.

Vin!

Two of the men cried out, blood pouring from their noses and ears before squirting out their eyes.

Vin! LET GO!

She cried out, and cold air filled her lungs. She was enmeshed with another conscience. Tangled. She'd gone too far. She knew better. She'd been trained. This type of connection could be permanent. Maybe deadly.

She fought her instinct to react out of fear. That way lay death. She had to retreat within her own mind and completely let go of the other's emotions. Something held her, wouldn't let go. Like trying to shut a door against the force of a thousand stars.

Struggle wasn't the answer.

Calm. She focused on her breathing. It was her breathing, had been all along. But those thoughts...no, memories, they weren't hers.

Focus.

The breathing regulated to a familiar pattern. She was back, but the residual effect of such emotion was devastating. She'd gone too far.

Sobs reached her ears. She was alive, but she didn't care.

Sadness and grief enveloped her. She rolled to her side, curled into a ball, and wept.

~

VIN DIDN'T KNOW HOW LONG SHE'D BEEN THERE, BUT THE tears had finally stopped. You couldn't touch another's emotions without experiencing some of it yourself, but this had been different. It wasn't like the usual empath connection; it was as though she had *been* that person. And something had happened. Something bad.

"Are you awake?"

She knew that voice. Or at least, she should. She was on her side, someplace soft and warm. She didn't want to remember why she was here.

"Vin." Armond.

She opened her eyes.

He knelt by the side of a bed and stared into her soul.

Panic shot through her when she realized her shields were down. She couldn't go back into that tortured mind, but she couldn't stop the connection. She waited for the horrific flood of power and pain, but it didn't come.

"It's all right. My emotions are completely blocked."

Emotions. Armond. Not an empty shell. A killer.

For the first time in her life, she had no words.

"I need to check your injuries. The damage was extensive, nearly fatal." Armond paused for so long she thought he was done. "In order to save you, I had to use my psi and heal you from the inside out. I wasn't expecting your empathic ability to be so...overpowering. We were both asleep when you connected. You won't feel anything this time."

She instinctively pulled away when he reached out for her. "I can't go there again."

He paused. "You will never go there again. I promise."

A tremendous grief descended upon her at the words. She couldn't define her feelings for him. He'd killed at least three people and yet...

"Do not fear me." His voice was flat, but there was an undercurrent. It was that thing that buzzed through her. That thing that was somehow this man.

She was so disconnected, detached, from her usual state of emotional equilibrium. A psychotic break. She needed sleep.

Armond's brows drew together. "I must ensure you have no further internal bleeding, and our med kit lacks the proper equipment. You will not die on my watch, nor by my touch." There was conviction in his words. And truth was, he could have killed her many times over, but instead, he'd healed her.

She forced herself to relax and nodded. There was nothing she could do in her present condition, and her gut said he could be trusted. Why she wanted to, she wasn't sure.

He placed one hand on hers, and the other on her neck. A gentle but firm touch that sent tendrils of pleasure darting through her.

Yes, it felt good. The sensation amplified, then simply vanished. An odd feeling, almost a vibration, surrounded her injured areas. After knowing what it was to be mentally connected to this man, the lack thereof was startling. A strange void.

"You'll be fine now. I had to effect one final repair in your artery, and another in the veins of your wrist. Sleep." He removed his touch, leaving cold empty space.

Fatigue quickly overcame her, she closed her eyes, and heard his foot falls moving away. "Wait." There would be nightmares tonight. Of that she was certain. "I don't want to be alone. This bed is huge. Not to mention it's yours. You can sleep on the other side." The words preceded the thought. Stupid.

There was a long pause before he responded. "I will sit for now." There was no emotion, but that buzz was there. An anchor in her state of detachment.

Vin woke to the sound of the door whooshing open. Armond entered, carrying a steaming mug. "I made you some fortified caff."

She sat up and slipped her bare legs off the bed, stretching her arms and rolling her shoulders before taking the cup. The back of her hand showed nothing more than patches of pink where the acid had eaten away at her skin. She stroked her neck and felt no imperfection. "You have impressive powers of healing."

"We are most fortunate it is one of my stronger abilities."

She sipped the caff, sweetened the way she liked it. "Thank you." She wore one of Armond's tees and nothing else. Interesting.

"I had to discard your clothing. I removed as much excess blood as I could, but you'll want to shower. Are you recovered sufficiently to continue our quest?"

"I think so." A quick check assured her that her shields were strong as ever, and she was energized. Strange that there had been no nightmares. "What time is it?"

"Nearly ten a.m. Primaera time. We need to open the box and determine our next objective."

"Yes, of course. Let's do that now, and I'll shower when we're underway." She rose to her feet and followed him to the galley. He had such a stunning physique, she couldn't help but imagine his hands on her. Nor could she stop seeing those faces. What had happened to those people?

The galley was spotless. It must have taken a lot to clean

that mess. "I'm sorry. It was stupid of me to take those flowers." She recalled copious amounts of blood.

"You thought they were beautiful and wanted them for the ship." There was an intensity to his gaze.

"That's about right. I'll be more careful."

Something had changed between them.

Armond retrieved the box from the counter and handed it to her.

"You didn't have to wait for me to open this."

"We're a team. We do this together."

Such simple words. Why did they grab her with such force?

The box warm to the touch, she unlocked the latches and opened the lid. Inside, a crystal glowed with the same light from the cave. A souvenir. Next to it lay a small scroll. Setting the box down, she retrieved the paper and unfurled it.

DECEPTION IS FICKLE WHEN THE ANSWER IS UNFAIR.

Lies not lies and truths untold.

High in the sky, floating in air, your next task is to the depths of despair.

"WELL THAT FIGURES." VIN PUSHED THE SCRAP AWAY.

"What does?"

"I'm guessing it has something to do with heights. You're claustrophobic, I don't do heights."

"You climbed that wall back in the cave without apparent stress."

"That was my limit."

"Heights do not affect me. I'm sure I can perform the task."

She scowled at him. "You really should watch those old episodes of this show. They'll find a way to put it on me."

"Why did you sign up for this?" Armond asked. "Knowing what you do and that your life could be at risk."

It was the first personal question he'd asked her. She crossed her arms and leaned against the counter. "Life can be terribly boring. I was in a holding pattern. Had been for a few years. I was ready for some excitement. That, and I didn't really think I'd get in, so I went for it. I admit, I had some trepidation when I was selected, but the application is binding. Since I couldn't do anything about it, I embraced it. And you had no choice?"

"That is correct."

Her feet were getting cold. "Marty, do you know our next destination?"

"Affirmative. It arrived as you were inspecting the contents of the box. We are to go to Omagar. I believe the weather will be extreme."

"Hot or cold?" Armond asked.

"Hot."

"Marty," Vin said, "did you know about the acid-spitting flowers?"

"Affirmative."

"Why didn't you warn us?" Vin asked.

"I'm quite sure I did."

"You did not," Armond said.

"I do not understand."

One of Armond's eyebrows twitched. Maybe.

"At this point I'm thinking we can't trust Marty," Vin said. "*Lies not lies and truths untold.* Come on. I'll check the nav coordinates, and then I'm going to shower and cook us a decent meal. You like stew?" Armond nodded. "I love stew. I'll make stew."

They crossed the hall to the bridge. Vin sat and pulled up

the coordinates Marty had stored. The cold of the leather on the back of her knees felt good. "Seems legit. It's four hours out."

Marty chimed for attention. "The media crew from station DAZL is requesting an interview."

"No thank you." Armond said.

"Can't decline. Part of the contract." Vin shrugged.

"Then why did he ask and not simply inform?"

He seemed truly perplexed. "Politeness, maybe? I don't know. Get us out of here so I can go shower. Marty, tell the crew we'll be with them in an hour. They can film us in the galley while I cook. More entertaining that way."

ARMOND SAT AT THE ISLAND, HANDS WRAPPED AROUND A CUP of caff, while Vin sorted out necessary ingredients, meat browning in a pan next to her. Why she took pleasure in creating meals from scratch, he couldn't fathom. Cooking the old way took longer. It did, however, allow one to savor the changing aromatic properties. And he had to admit, the aroma was enticing. And she did take pleasure in the activity. Even now, she quietly sang some song about a lover on a distant planet.

Her back was to him, her ample curves on display.

He didn't know how much she'd seen when their psi had connected, but it was enough to be afraid of him. And their psi *had* connected. Had done so in a way he would never again allow. Vin had somehow breached his defenses and lived. Saving her had been a close call, and he'd nearly lost her. Twice. The thought was disturbing on a visceral level.

"Are you okay?" Vin's voice rang with concern.

Armond met her gaze. "Why do you ask?"

"I don't know. I sensed something."

Sensed his reaction to the thought of losing her. He couldn't look away from her eyes of near black. His shields were fully intact. How had she sensed that? This was a dangerous direction for him to be contemplating. "I am fine, Vin. It was nothing."

She wiped her hands on a dish towel and eyed him skeptically. "If you say so."

ARMOND WORE HIS USUAL BLANK MASK, BUT VIN KNEW something had just occurred. That resonance he caused in her body had gone into hyperdrive. There was something to his nothing.

Marty interrupted their staring contest. "The media crew is ready for you."

"Activate the galley cams," Vin said.

"They've been active for the past thirty minutes, darling." There was no mistaking the twang of the DAZL reporter Mac Wendorn.

"Thanks for letting us know." Vin hid her annoyance. Had they revealed anything that would be useful to the other contestants? She'd been tempted to talk to Armond about the deaths. That could have been disastrous. They'd have to figure out how to ensure privacy, moving forward.

"Glad to see you two crazy kids made it off Altaria in one piece. Should have seen the betting pools pinging on that one. Money will be exchanging hands with this airing."

"What were my odds of survival?" Vin asked.

"Seventy-thirty you weren't going to make it. That's one nasty flower." Mac leaned forward into the cam. "In fact, you're looking pretty damn fine for all that blood."

"The ships AI provided a neutralizing agent for the acid," Armond said.

"Yeah, but that don't heal the skin. What d'you two do?

Hey Carl," Mac called to someone over his shoulder. "Cue up the galley feed for yesterday."

Vin turned back to her stew. She wasn't sure she wanted to see this. The fact that they'd been watched for the past thirty minutes made her angry. She picked up the bottle of Kartoosh and couldn't recall if she'd added it already or not. She blew out a breath and put in half of her usual. Split the difference.

"Ok, he's got the neutralizing agent." Mac was providing a blow-by-blow of the feed. It was one of his signature moves. "Looks like he's got all the splatter points. Hard to tell with all that blood. What's he doing now?"

Vin couldn't resist and turned to see.

Mac had the feed playing on holo-vid. A nearly life-sized Armond leaned over Vin with one hand each on her arm and neck.

A phantom touch whispered on her skin, and she had an overwhelming desire to reach out to Armond.

"I am healing her from the inside out," Armond said matter-of-factly.

"You can do that?" Mac whistled.

A few moments later, the media crew was whooping and hollering as Armond undressed her insanely fast.

"Oh, darling, you got some nice curves."

Vin turned to Armond. "You washed me here?" She wasn't sure why it shocked her.

"The metal surface of the counter was the most effective and sanitary location. I did not know we were being recorded."

More cheering came from the media. "That's quite a nice touch you have there, big boy."

On the holo, Armond used a galley sponge and systemati-cally wiped away blood. At first his motions were purely functional, but with each stroke there was a noticeable shift.

His actions progressing from mechanical to a gentle sweep. Thoughtful even. Desire washed over her as she imagined his touch.

She didn't mind that her nudity would be seen across the galaxy; she was proud of her curves. But she wished that the moment had stayed private for Armond's sake.

He placed his hands on her again and closed his eyes for another round of healing. After a few minutes, she cried out and curled into a ball, weeping.

The visceral memory of his anguish still hurt. She watched the entire process until he'd gently picked her up and carried her out of the galley.

"Aw, ain't that sweet. You two going to be our next official couple?" Mac asked.

"No." Armond stood. "My only interest in Vin is in winning this farce." He turned and left, his lie echoing in her soul.

"That boy has some issues," Mac said laughing. "Think you can warm him up?"

Vin put on her best flirty smile for the vid. "A girl can certainly try." Decent ratings were important for the contest. Ties for first place had been broken in the past due to a pair's popularity with the viewers. Armond's cold demeanor could turn them into a fan favorite. The fans loved assholes. Even if that's not what they were.

"Hey, Mac," Vin said, laying on the charm. "How about a heads up when you're filming? You are supposed to let us know."

He smiled, rolling a toothpick around the side of his mouth. "Sure thing, sugar."

Armond returned shortly after Mac and his crew signed off. "We won't have to worry about the vidbot feed."

"Why not?"

"I've disconnected them. No filming or recording until I reconnect."

"Good thinking. It'll piss off the corporation, but the viewers will love it. For a while. We need to make sure we keep them happy with what they can see."

"And what makes them happy?" He returned to his seat at the island.

"Things going wrong. People arguing." Sex.

"I don't argue."

Vin dished out two servings of stew and set them down. "There is another viewer favorite."

"Which is?"

"Romance."

His ice blues snapped up to her face. "Intimacy is not an option."

He'd been pretty damn intimate when he cleaned her. "We could just fake it. It might make the difference between winning and losing."

She grabbed a bottle of water for each of them, and sat down next to him.

"It is not a good idea."

There was a familiar resonance surrounding the words.

"Armond, what happened with the girl and those men?" The question was out before she processed the thought. Too late to take it back, she waited.

The man had a way of going preternaturally still, and his gaze was on her. The silence was beyond uncomfortable before he answered. "The occurrences were isolated, unintentional, and have not happened since."

She'd figured that out from his sheer horror at their deaths. "Do you know wh—"

"I do not wish to discuss it."

She nodded. It was enough. For now. He wasn't a monster, but he had a problem.

He scooped up a large bite of stew and blew on it before taking it into his mouth. The movement was oddly titillating.

She gave him a few moments to process the flavors. "What do you think?"

"Delicious."

"Thank you." They ate in silence.

When they'd finished, Armond surprised her by offering to clean up.

"Really?"

"I am perfectly capable of contributing. Since I cannot cook such as you, I will clean up."

"Great. I'll go and check our approach to Omagar."

Armond took their bowls to the sink, and she watched him a moment. The man epitomized hidden depths. The more she knew, the more she wanted to know.

CHAPTER 5

"*W*hat do you mean 'there's no land'?" Vin monitored their approach to Omagar.

"I mean the planet surface is covered in water," Marty replied.

"How are we supposed to retrieve the box?"

"I am unable to answer that question."

"For an AI, you sure have a wide range of emotional vocal patterns."

"Turns out I have even more than that," Marty said. Behind her, a tall bald man walked onto the bridge.

Vin jumped to her feet, heart pounding. Octiron had planted more than one stowaway over the years. There was the slightest shimmer around the man's body. "Marty?" Vin asked.

Good-looking and muscled, the man smiled and spun in a slow circle. "What do you think?"

"Not bad," Vin said. "Why haven't you materialized before?"

"I didn't realize I had holographic abilities. I recently gained access to the programs."

Armond walked onto the bridge a moment later and stood in Marty.

"Excuse you!" Marty stepped to the left and glared at Armond.

"Is a holographic form necessary?" Armond asked.

Marty's hip jutted out to the left. "It adds flair, and you two need some." He flicked his wrist at Armond and blinked out.

"I have plenty of flair, thank you very much," Vin said. She turned to Armond, "We have a complication."

Armond slid into the captain's chair. "What is it?"

"Marty just informed me there's no land on Omagar. It's a water planet." Vin retook her seat.

"Marty, pull up a holo on the planet's information," Armond said.

An aquamarine orb came into view on the projection. To the right was a list of statistics, facts, and figures regarding the planet.

"Hey," Vin slapped the console. "Not five minutes ago you told me you didn't have anything else."

"I do not recall that request," Marty's electronic voice replied.

"Liar," Vin said.

"I am incapable of lying." He stood behind her now, hands on hips.

She flipped him off with thumb, index, and pinky extended.

"What does that mean?" Armond asked.

"Let's just say it's not very polite. First thing I asked him when I got here was for information and he said he didn't have any."

"I am incapable of—"

"Oh, shut up." Vin leaned closer to read the data. "Breathable oxygen. Seriously high saline content in the water. And algae. There's thousands of varieties of micro-organisms. Marty, are any of those things dangerous to us?"

"Negative."

She looked at Armond and shrugged. "He's right about the water. Completely covered, but surprisingly shallow in most places."

"Very shallow," Armond agreed. "The planet is nearly five times the size of Earth and has less than two percent of the water content."

"Where's Earth?" Vin scrolled through the data.

"Back in my own galaxy."

"Is it pretty?"

"I suppose it would be considered as such."

"But, what do you think?" She flashed him a smile, and realized it was something he had never done.

"I do not think in such terms."

"You sound like Marty." But he was no computer.

The image on the hologram rotated, and a red dot blinked.

"I believe this is where you will find your next objective," Marty said.

They were coming in on the opposite side of the planet. She ran the calculations through the nav. "We're thirty minutes out." She turned to Armond, "Maybe this isn't the up challenge but the down. I assume we can simply hover over the water's surface?"

"Will do," Armond adjusted their approach.

"I'm afraid that is not correct." Marty said. His voice had an odd inflection to it, and his holographic form stood inspecting its fingernails.

"We should have no problem maintaining a stationary position." Armond scanned through a screen on the console.

"Our minimum distance from the surface is three hundred and twelve feet."

"There is no reason why we can't—"

"It's not the ship," Vin interrupted. "It's the contest, right Marty?"

"That is correct."

"Is the ship equipped with a shuttle?" Armond asked.

"Yes, but you are not allowed to use it."

"How do we get down?" Vin found the AI increasingly annoying.

"I suggest you take an inventory of the contents of locker sixteen in the cargo bay." Marty sounded downright cheerful.

"I'm starting to really not care for this little AI piece of shit." She had to laugh when the holograph that was Marty momentarily morphed into a large brown pile of excrement. Vin stood and stretched her arms over her head, then folded forward and touched her toes. When she straightened, Armond watched her with singular intensity.

"You should try it. Feels good."

"I get a sufficiency of exercise."

"I noticed." And he'd touched nearly every inch of her. She shuddered at the thought. Pity she didn't remember any of it.

They made their way down to the cargo bay. Unlike the rest of the ship, this was bare bones. Lockers lined one wall, and they went to number sixteen.

Inside was a harness.

"That's it?" Vin peered closer. "Ah." Coiled at the bottom was a white filament. She reached down and retrieved it. "How much you want to bet this is just long enough?"

"Is it strong enough to hold me?"

"Honey, this can hold far more than you. It's called Trache Filament. They use it to make orbital lifts, among other things."

"We need to measure it." Armond fingered the thin material.

It took them a while, but they determined it was approximately six hundred and fifteen feet. "Convenient." Vin recoiled the rope.

"At least you don't have to go down," Armond said. "I can rig up a pulley, lower myself, and retrieve it with my psi."

"I hope so, but I'm not buying it. Not yet." It was too easy. She knew how this worked.

They returned to the bridge. On the viewscreen, clouds covered the planet. They descended as close as they could above their target, and set a stationary position.

"Wow." Vin amplified the image. The water glowed in tiny rippling waves. "Bioluminescence."

"I believe we are directly over the object," Marty reported. "It appears to be fifteen feet under the surface. It is also surrounded by the crystals found in the caves on Omagar."

"The pink ones or blue?" Armond asked.

"Pink," Marty replied.

"Those crystals mean you can't use your psi, doesn't it?" Vin asked, her gut tightening.

Armond nodded.

"Fifteen feet isn't bad. You can use a breather helmet," Vin said.

"Negative," Marty said in a sing-song voice weirdly reminiscent of Candi. "Not permitted during this task."

"Fine. You can swim, right? Assuming the critters living in that soup don't kill you." She went for humor.

Armond turned to her. His face was the same mask as always, and yet something subtle clued her in. She closed her eyes and blew out a breath as the fear climbed up her gut. "You can't swim."

"Correct."

It had to be like this. It's why everyone loved the show. She imagined trying to descend on that filament. "I don't have the upper body strength to get down and back up again."

"I do."

"And there it is. The shot the network is looking for. You harnessed in and holding me. They're evil." But like the sponge scene, this would be ratings gold. She couldn't think about it. Simply had to do it. She eyed his strong arms and broad chest. That's what she'd focus on. Being in Armond Nolde's arms. "Let's get this over with. I'm going to put on some shorts."

"I'll meet you in the airlock."

Vin changed into shorts and a short-sleeved top. The floor was cold on her bare feet.

Armond waited for her. Surprisingly, he wore shorts as well, and a black tee shirt. Legs for days. They fastened the harness to him. The damn thing was nearly too small, but they got it secured.

Vin grabbed a handhold and opened the outer door. A wave of damp heat hit her in the face. She forced herself to peek over the edge to the water below. Her stomach dropped, and she fought panic. She spun and faced Armond. She could do this. Had to do it. Her fear would be her strength.

Armond fastened the line to an anchor point.

Her heart hammered as he readied the pulley.

He stood and faced her, arms crossed and muscles bulging. Good, strong muscles that were going to keep her alive. She hoped.

"You appear to be in distress," Armond said.

She scowled at him. "Not my idea of a good time."

He gave her his standard curt nod. "I've rigged up an extra strap. You'll be able to sit on it. You'll need to wrap yourself around me while I secure it. I'd prefer you keep your arms and legs around my body as an added measure of security."

She burst out laughing just as a vidbot buzzed by outside. If this were any other man, she'd accuse him of manipulating the situation, but this was Armond, and that was simply logical.

"Are you ready?" Marty stood leaning against the bulkhead, arms and ankles crossed.

"Almost," Vin said. "I have to jump."

"I could simply lift you with psi," Armond said.

"Better this way. Ratings."

Armond dropped his arms and widened his stance. The vidbot zoomed in closer.

The viewers were going to love this. She wiped her palms on her shirt. "On the count of three. One, two…three." She took four steps and leapt, wrapping her legs around his waist on impact.

He caught her easily and had the strap under her ass in no time.

"Try your weight on it."

Vin loosened the grip on her legs and settled into the sling. "Looks like we're good." She was inches away from his face, that hint of spice and musk surrounding her.

The pesky vidbot zoomed around them like a gnat on Tibor, spending a ridiculous amount of time on her backside before popping up by their faces.

Armond reached out with insane speed and sent it flying out the airlock.

Being wrapped around him like this had that odd resonance humming inside her. She hooked her ankles together behind Armond's back, and couldn't resist the urge to take hold of his pony tail and twirl it around her fingers. The bot was hovering off to the left, soaking it all up.

"I'd tell you to smile since we're being recorded, but I

know better. You have really soft hair. I'd love to braid it for you sometime."

Without warning, his psi enveloped them as it had in the cave on Altaria, and they lifted off the floor and drifted out the airlock.

Vin plastered herself to Armond and buried her face in his neck. She was simultaneously terrified and enraptured by a feeling of intense pleasure. She breathed him in.

Gravity returned as he eased off the psi and let them down with the pulley.

"Probably best to keep your eyes closed," Armond said in her ear.

The pleasure had tapered off substantially, but his psi did things to her. Things she liked. She remembered the orgasm she'd had when he'd healed her. Keeping her eyes closed was definitely the way to go. She tightened her grip and inhaled. He smelled so damn good.

The constant motion of his strong arms as he lowered them was almost a caress.

Without thinking, she pressed her lips to his skin and licked.

His movement faltered, and they dropped.

She screamed, and held tight as they fell.

Intense concern for her safety washed over her. Armond's concern. For her. A surge of his power erupted and she instinctively redirected it, felt it as it flowed around them and into the water below.

They slammed to a halt as an explosion of salty water drenched them from beneath. She opened her eyes and looked down to find they were less than a foot from the water's surface.

"Was that my fault?"

His face was expressionless, but his eyes shone with intensity. "Yes."

"It felt good, though, didn't it? When I tasted you."

The vidbot zipped around them, this time out of Armond's reach.

"We connected again just now. Your power didn't hurt us. Or me." She spoke too low for the bot to pick up. "It was nice." No horrid memories.

She felt his shields slip. Damn if he didn't want to kiss her.

"You know," Vin said louder, "there's a very real chance we won't survive this."

"There's a good chance we won't survive a kiss," he whispered. They had two conversations going on, one for the show, and another for them.

"I'm willing to take that chance." She didn't wait for an answer as she pressed her lips to his.

There was a moment of hesitation before he devoured her, his psi engulfing them, ricocheting around her energy centers. Dancing, resonating, as a lifetime of longing poured into her.

He stopped abruptly. His face more animated than she'd ever seen, with amazement written in those eyes. A background buzz built within him.

Another surge of psi blasted her muscles, causing a brief paralysis before she deflected it. She sucked in a breath a moment later.

Amazement had turned to terror on Armond's face. "Tell me you're ok."

"Yeah, I'm okay. What is that?"

"That is the reason I will never kiss you again."

"Um, yeah, no. That doesn't work for me." What he did to her, that kiss. Going backwards wasn't an option. She could fix this.

"Pardon," Marty said. "I hate to interrupt your moment of intimacy, especially since the viewers will be eating this up, but there is a rather large disturbance heading your way. It will be at this location in approximately four point three minutes. I suggest you expedite your progress."

"What kind of disturbance?" Armond asked.

"It is wave of increasing size. Apparently it is a common periodic phenomena on this world. It does, in fact, account for the anomalous orbit of the planet and the height limitation of the ship."

"What do you mean a wave?" Vin asked. "The water is shallow." She glanced down and her heart stopped. "Oh no. It's getting shallower."

"That is correct. The wave is pulling the water into the crest it's forming. It's quite impressive. The ship is at a safe distance. You, however, are not."

"Shit." She tightened her legs and lifted so Armond could unfasten the sling. "You sure you can reach me?"

"I will reach you." His voice had gone cold again. Emotionless. The strap fell to the side.

"Just so you know," Vin said, noting that the bot was close. "That was not the last time you are going to kiss me."

She let go and dropped. The water was almost too hot.

"You're directly over the object," Armond called down.

She took four deep breaths, held the last, and dove. The water stung her eyes, but the visibility was good. Too good. They were in trouble. The crystals weren't just surrounding the box. She grabbed it and pushed off back to the surface. She wiped her eyes and held up the box. "We have a problem."

His psi wrapped around her. Her breath caught as pleasure rippled through her, but he couldn't get a grip on her. Not with the crystal-encased box she held in her hand.

"You are correct," Armond said. "A very large problem."

Vin preferred the previous look of amazement to the

emotion written on Armond's face now. It was fear. "What do we do?"

There was a long pause before he shouted down. "Drop it. We're done."

"Wrong answer. Try again."

His anger was somehow comforting as he called down to her. "Can you read my feelings now, holding the box?"

A wave of concern hit her hard. "Loud and clear."

"Your psi isn't affected by the crystal. Perhaps I can use it to bring you up."

"I can't do that shit with my *psi*. I'm an empath, remember?"

"You can't do it, but maybe I can. It means you'll be fully exposed again. To me. Are you ready for that?"

"I do not wish to cause any further duress," Marty was downright giddy, "but you have approximately thirty-eight seconds."

Vin spun around and felt as though she'd been punched in the gut. There was a wall well over one hundred feet high approaching them. As she kicked to stay afloat, she touched bottom. She wasn't floating anymore. The water pulled at her legs. "Armond!"

"Give me your psi!"

She had no idea what that meant, but she dropped every shield she had and tried to walk toward him. The familiar psi wrapped around her, struggling to grab hold. He had her, then slipped. Had her again, lifted, and slipped again. This time the retreating water sucked her legs out from under her and she fell face down, slamming into the sandy bottom, clawing for a hold.

The water sucked her out.

"Don't let go of the box," Armond shouted, following overhead. "And drop the rest of your defenses."

Anger burst within. If she had any defenses up, she wasn't

in control of them. An old trick from her training days came to mind.

She screamed for all she was worth. It worked. Whatever was left shattered, and she was awash in Armond's thoughts. He tried to compartmentalize every emotion going through him, but keeping her safe was first and foremost.

Armond's mind skittered across everything he'd been, everything he was, everything he might be.

A couple flashed before her. A dark haired, roguish male and auburn-haired woman. Smiling, laughing.

She nearly dropped the box as she rose off the sand, fumbled then caught it. She crashed into Armond and he shouted. "Marty, go! Get us out of here. Marty!" He yanked on the pulley. They were ascending, but not fast enough.

Nearly clear of the crest, the wall of water slammed into them. Armond had her by the waist, but the force of the water was relentless. No air in her lungs, she had to breathe. It was a battle she couldn't win. Her chest spasmed and her lungs filled with water. They broke the surface and Armond squeezed her. She coughed up mouthful after mouthful as they rose above the wave top.

The ship did a rapid descent to scoop them up, and her lungs were on fire as they slammed into the airlock floor, her arms curled around the box. Nausea swept over her as she continued coughing. The water was bitter and mixed with bile. But they were in. With the box.

Armond's barriers returned, and she was overwhelmed with the emptiness left behind.

"Are you all right?" he asked.

She nodded. "Will be." Her voice was broken and raspy. He helped her to her feet.

Armond secured the outer latch, and they moved into the interior of the ship and headed for the galley. Anger radiated off the man in waves.

"Marty!" Armond's bellow scared the crap out of her as they entered the kitchen area along with the vidbot.

"Glad to see you made it back in one piece." Marty sat on the counter, feet dangling and tapping a rapid beat. "What can I help you with?"

"What the hells was that about?" The stools around the island scattered in different directions, slamming against the first thing in their path. "You damn near got us killed, you spineless, fucktard, useless piece of AI garbage."

A blast of Armond's psi ripped out, and the island did a weird crumpling thing and sagged along the middle, melting into composite metal. Every loose item on the counters rattled.

Anger had turned to pure rage.

"Armond! Stop!" Vin took his rogue energy and deflected it straight down to the planet below.

The silence was deafening as they faced each other.

He stepped closer, studying her. "What did you do?"

"I redirected. Sent everything you had down to the planet. Same thing I did out there."

"That would explain the crater that formed approximately twenty-five meters into the planet's surface," Marty said. "Underwater. The force required for such an impact is most impressive."

"Twenty-five meters?" Impressive wasn't the word. This was a man, not a machine.

Armond remained frozen. It occurred to her that the man didn't know *how* to feel. He'd shut it down years ago to protect others. Until now.

"No one has been able to contain that burst of energy. Ever." His voice was low.

Everything snapped into place. "That's how...those people."

The damn vidbot was buzzing around.

Armond reached out his hand and the bot froze, captured by his psi. A moment later, sparks shot out of it as it shrank into a crumpled ball.

He nodded.

Vin stepped close to him and placed her palm over his heart. "That's why you shut everything down. The reason you're so damn cold."

He lowered his hand over hers. There was longing in those pale eyes. And skepticism. Wonderment. And, best of all, hope.

"Let me help you, Armond. Let me teach you how to feel."

His eyes closed.

"You want this, Armond. You *deserve* this." She reached up with her free hand and cupped his cheek. "This burst of anger was a gift. You will not hurt me."

He opened his eyes and tilted his head. There was a softening around the eyes and mouth. He wanted this as much as she did.

"I can redirect it."

His expression slayed her. His whole life had been lived in fear of hurting others, so he'd withdrawn. So alone.

"Trust me." She rose on her toes and pressed a kiss to his cheek, his chin, inching closer she finally reached his lips. Wrapping her arms around his neck, she pulled him tight. "Let me in."

He did. Opening to her tongue. Afraid. Ravenous.

She felt the power surge coming, but she knew what to do with it. No resistance, a simple redirection down to the planet. After the initial pulse, it tempered off, leaving them blissfully alone. Together.

KISSING VIN WAS THE MANIFESTATION OF EVERY SUPPRESSED

SABINE PRIESTLEY

desire he'd ever had rolled up with forbidden fantasy. A dream that was real.

Her curves beckoned to be explored without the damn clothes.

He pulled back with a groan. "You're sure you'll be all right?"

"I'll be fine, but I could be better." She smiled up at him, and his breath caught as she palmed his erection.

Never had he wanted anything this much, never allowed himself to entertain the possibility, but he had to ensure her safety. "You can handle any surges?"

"Like pouring water down a drain. I faltered a few times out there before I realized what was happening." She nodded toward the airlock. "But I have it now. I can feel when it's coming. There's an energy signature."

He didn't need any more of an invitation. He'd keep his psi in check, but she was right. He deserved this.

They both did. And he would not overthink it. He placed his hand on the small of her back and steered her toward the bedroom.

"May I be of further assistance?" Marty chimed in. "A replacement vidbot has been dispatched. The media are asking for supplementation from your com units in the meantime. Everyone wants to know what you did to the island."

"Fuck them," Armond said.

Vin grinned, and picked up the pace next to him.

He closed the door behind them and checked his com to ensure there were no active sensors. He looked at Vin and held up one finger. "I'll be right back."

"Join me in the shower. Need to de-grunge." Vin pulled her shirt over her head.

Gods, she was spectacular.

He spun and headed for the bridge. Reaching under the

console, he got down on his back and popped off the casing to access the cabling and fuses. Marty crouched on the floor next to him. "Is there a problem I am unaware of?"

"I'd say you're aware of it." He found the circuits he needed, and pulled the plug on the AI system. "But not any more." Should have done that a long time ago. He stood and made his way back to Vin.

Vin. He fought his instinct to analyze the situation. He was willing to take this for what it was. Whatever it turned out to be.

In the bedroom, he stripped off his wet clothes, tossing them on a pile with Vin's. A moment later, he stepped into the shower behind her. This was something he'd never even imagined.

Vin stood with her eyes closed, rinsing her hair. The deep blue of her skin was beautiful. She finished, and smiled coyly over her shoulder. "What are you waiting for?"

"Just savoring the moment. I've never showered with a woman." Never much of anything with a woman. Not since Dareena.

The look on her face showed just how much she'd got of that. "Come here."

He stepped into the hot steaming water. Vin lathered up a sponge and began to wash him. She caressed, stroked, petted, every inch.

Sensory overdose. He closed his eyes and reveled in more physical contact than he'd ever had. More than he'd ever expected. The impossibility of this reality making the moment dream-like and surreal.

"You are amazing." Vin's voice was heavy with lust. She knelt down and finished with his lower legs, his desire bobbing inches from her face. She dropped the sponge and wrapped her hand around his shaft. "Vin..." He slapped his palms against the wall and rode the exquisite sensation of her lips on him. She sucked and licked and scrapped her teeth along the ridge. She found her rhythm and cupped his balls, and he came hard and fast.

She continued sucking, milking him dry. His psi pinged erratically. Almost as if struggling. Everything about this experience both foreign and natural at the same time.

He grabbed her arms and lifted. It was probably best she'd taken the initial edge off.

He turned off the water. "Come. Time to return the favor."

Thirty seconds later, Vin lay in the center of the bed on her back, one knee in the air and a sexy sweet smile on her face. "Don't make me wait."

Thoughts battled for attention, but he refused to think. This moment, this place in time, would not be defiled with guilt or doubt. She wanted this as much as he did, and he knew enough to satisfy.

She unabashedly drank him in from head to toe. The ladies that served him did so with, at most, his pants at his knees. Cold. Sterile. As instructed.

"What's wrong?" she halted his mental downward spiral.

"Nothing. You're stunning." He extended his psi, coating her in his desire.

Her eyes widened, and her skin radiated a bioluminescent glow.

Armond took his time, then lay next to her. There was never going to be another first. "You're glowing."

She rolled to her side, propped on one elbow, and began stroking him everywhere. Light teasing touches. "It's a physiological reaction of my people when we're…aroused."

He leaned over and kissed his way from her jaw to her chest before taking an amble nipple into his mouth. Her moan of pleasure matched his own, and he massaged the other breast. This was a feast of the senses, and they were both devouring the experience.

He rolled on top of her, and switched to the enchantingly pink flesh of her other nipple.

"Don't stop." That stereophonic resonance of her voice played his insides.

He kept his psi in check. Locked. The sheer physicality of this time was almost too much. There were things he couldn't think about. Not now.

She trailed her fingers across his lips, and he felt it in his groin, the touch of another being a nearly foreign experience.

She smiled up at him and moved her body in a way that beckoned. "You know what I need."

He positioned himself at her entrance. He'd never thought he'd do this again. A wall of emotion and energy hit him and expanded outward, his psi enveloping her along with it.

Vin placed her hands on his face and kept her sexy smile. "See? We got this."

The destructive surge poured away without a trace. In the next breath, Armond slid home.

CHAPTER 6

*T*here were orgasms, and then there was this. The heat of Armond's body was sublime against Vin's skin as the pleasure rolled around her senses. She'd had her share of good-looking men before, but nothing like Armond Nolde. Not only was he sinfully gorgeous, he was pure muscle. She could spend days running her hands over that ass.

His look was intense as he gazed down at her.

"I've never seen you smile." She wanted to see it.

"I've spent my life blocking emotion."

The tragedy of those words nearly made her weep. "I want to change that." She traced his lips with a finger. "Life should be lived with a smile on your face."

Coming off the post-orgasm high, she realized that his psi was absent. Held in check. Which was a pity, considering the effect it had on her.

Staring into those pained blue eyes, she found that she wanted it. His psi, and so much more. But what about him? Could a man so damaged truly give himself to anyone? To her?

Yes. It was a gut-level response, but he was going to have to believe. Which meant she needed to convince him. She reached up and ran her fingers through his thick hair. "Sadly, I think it's time we find out what's next. 'In, out, up, down.' The cave was probably in. I suppose this last could be either up or down, depending on how you spin it."

He tilted his hips, burrowing deeper inside her. "It is sad. All right, let's do it."

She smiled. "I hope you say that a lot."

His eyes were smiling as he slid out of her.

After dressing, they returned to the galley. The island was a total loss. "You are extremely powerful," Vin said. "I'm fairly certain I can help you control your anger. Avoid the outbursts all together."

"Others have tried. All have failed."

"Until now. No one knew how to redirect it before me."

He gazed into her soul, a mixture of hope and disbelief playing across his features. And that play, that visible play of emotion, was something new for him. Joy didn't begin to describe the thrill rushing through her.

"Armond, you can now experience the joys of our...physicality." Vin traced his lips with her finger. She liked doing that. Thumbing his lower lip, she waited for the day he'd bite.

"Sex," Armond said.

"Making love. Anger is a valid component of our lives, our being. You shouldn't live in fear of that. I can help you control your psychic outbursts."

"Sounds like I'd have to get angry a lot."

"We'll start the groundwork." She turned back to the galley. "Marty, can we get the island fixed?"

"Marty can't hear you."

"What'd you do?"

"I unplugged him." Armond wore the faintest hint of a smile.

"Ha. And there it is. Our anger management object. Better fire him up."

"Let's open the box first. He'll already know what's in it by the time he's back online."

She scanned the counter. "Going to have to find it." They eventually located the box, wedged between the oven and a storage unit on the floor.

It had a crack that crossed the top, and one corner was smashed.

"Pity. It's still pretty, though. Let's hope the parchment isn't damaged."

Flipping the release, she opened the lid. Inside lay another stone. A radiant red gem.

"Beautiful," Vin said.

"We should turn it into a necklace for you."

It would make a lovely piece. She removed the scroll and smoothed it out on the counter. "Looks like we're headed for a planet called Setara Blue." She let go and it rolled back into a tube. Removing her com, she projected a star map and did a search. "That figures. It's in outlander territory."

"Outlanders?" Armond asked.

She sensed his confusion. "Yeah, they're lawless. Generally troublemakers. Not good. Why?"

"And they have a presence here?" He ignored her question.

"They patrol and protect the sector just outside the boundaries of the Central Alliance. Why? Have you heard of them?"

"Seems unlikely they'd be here and in my own galaxy. Any identifying characteristics?"

"A tattoo. It's the constellation of their territory." She felt his familiarity with them. "How is that possible?"

"I have no idea, but I suspect we're going to find out. I'll get Marty back online and we'll head out."

Armond lay on the floor and reconnected Marty's power before taking his seat.

Vin slipped in next to him at the navigation console.

"What's our status, Marty?" Armond pulled up the ships sensor display.

Silence.

"Marty, are you there?" Vin asked.

A prolonged burst of static blasted through the speakers with enough volume to vibrate the seat.

"Ow, stop that!" Vin slapped her hands over her ears until it stopped. "Don't ever do that again."

The silence was deafening.

"Come on, Marty," Vin coaxed. "Armond didn't mean anything by disconnecting you."

"It was rude," the AI finally replied.

"I was angry because you were being a...dick," Armond said.

Vin sensed that the vocabulary was outside of his norm. What must it be like to allow emotional expression for the first time in decades? "You did nearly get us killed," she chided.

"Nearly being the operative word." Marty snapped. He materialized with arms crossed, and pouted like a child.

"Truce, boys. We have a mission to finish." Vin pulled up the nav display. "We'll be there in about seven hours. Marty, please alert us to any nearby ships."

"Perhaps."

"I suggest we eat and get some sleep," Vin said. "It's been a long day." Not that "day" meant anything in space. One world's cycle around the local star was meaningless.

And sleep meant bed. She glanced at Armond, who was already looking at her lips.

She wanted to kiss him. Now.

"Biometric readings on both of you are elevated. It

suggests arousal. Am I to understand you have consummated your relationship? Is that why you disengaged me? Our sponsors would be very interested in that development."

"That's none of your business," Armond said.

"Of course it's my business. If you will refer to the contract, section two, paragraph—"

"You want me to disengage you again?" His anger pinged, and Vin's soothed him with a calming effect. His psi was still absent. "Come on. Let's eat."

Armond followed her into the galley. "We can't ensure our privacy unless we disconnect Marty."

A buzz crackled from the speakers.

"It's the way the game is played, Armond." Vin placed various ingredients on the counter, missing the workspace the island had provided.

"Can I help?" Armond leaned against the replicator, arms crossed.

"No. Just the company is good."

"Cooking relaxes you, doesn't it?"

"Yes." As did his presence, but without the connection they shared via his psi, it was an oddly empty experience. "You said you didn't know your parents. How is that?"

"I was placed in an orphanage on Sandaria shortly after my birth. I don't know anything about my origins."

"Any interest in trying to find out?"

Armond picked up a succulent dark purple pixberry and bit into it. "When I was young, I felt betrayed. I didn't want to know parents that hadn't wanted me. I simply didn't think about it."

"Foster parents?"

"I wasn't an open or loving child. The orphanage suited me."

"But you weren't completely detached. That girl..."

Armond's shoulders lowered a fraction. "Her name was

Dareena. She was my first. And aside from oral satisfaction from professionals, my last since you."

"You've only—"

"Had intercourse twice? Yes."

All the thoughts in her mind piled up in a tangled, derailed, mess.

"I was seventeen at the time. I'd begun having power surges a few months earlier, but didn't know what they were. The anomaly of her death and its circumstances brought me to the attention of the Portal Masters. Celibacy is a requirement of the order, which suited me fine after what had happened.

"The guild recognized my power and took me in. Trained me. It was during my initiation that I killed the three Portal Masters. Having seen it first hand, they understood the nature of the force. I was never again allowed into the inner sanctum and would never be a portal master, but they were good to me. They taught me how to contain my psi by living a life without emotion. They provided an education and military training.

It was ten years before I discovered I could allow a woman to service me safely as long as I remained detached."

The crushing weight of such a solitary existence made it difficult to breathe. Her existence was the total opposite.

Vin placed her palms on the cool surface and took a deep breath. His past was literally agony for her.

"Are you upset?" Armond asked.

She turned to face him. A week ago, all she would have seen was a cold, detached man. But she knew him better now. Could read the subtle signs of his internal battle. "I'm stunned. I hurt for the life you've missed."

"I have had a decent life."

"A lonely life. And now you're keeping your psi from me. Why?"

He reached out and ran his knuckles along her jawline. "Intimacy is not a language I know how to speak."

"That has nothing to do with your psi. I can tell the instant you pull back. You did it in bed earlier, and you've held it in check ever since." Something was eating at this man. Something major. "Talk to me."

∿

THE PSI CONNECTION HAD BEEN COMPLETELY UNEXPECTED, but there was no denying the potential for the psi-mate bond with this woman. A bond Armond had spent his life avoiding any possibilities of, knowing it to be impossible. But Vin had somehow breached his defenses, been exposed to his power surges, and lived.

Could it be due to their bonding potential?

She looked at him with such open desire and concern. "What aren't you saying, Armond?"

"The connection you feel. It is the interaction between your psi and mine."

She shook her head. "I don't get the psi thing."

"It manifests in you as your empathic abilities. You may be capable of more, with training. The point is, that connection is indicative of the bond between psi-mates."

Her skin began to glow as it had in bed. Thin lines, rivers of light, pulsating across every visible inch.

He took her hand, such a simple thing, and yet an intimacy such as he'd never thought possible.

Intimacy. It was a language he'd have to learn if this was more than fantasy. Hope and desire were foreign things to him, and along with them came the surge and release of his psi.

Vin deflected it easily and stepped closer, the corner of

her lips turned up. Their psi entwined in an ethereal dance. One of pleasure and promise.

"Tell me about psi-mates. What does it mean, exactly?"

"The bonding process is psi and bodies combined. It is sexual by nature. Pure energy. And permanent."

Their psi wound around each other, tightening further. This was an ecstasy many never experienced.

A low moan escaped Vin's perfect lips.

He met her gaze. "Are you certain about this? We will bond if I make love to you again. Psi-mates. That's a one-way trip."

Vin moved her body in a way that screamed desire and sensuality. "Armond, I'm already there. These ripples of light? They're because of you. Not because you turn me on, but because I love you."

The words hit him with the force of a Sandarian summer storm.

Love.

Vin tilted her head. "Say it."

He smiled, and her eyes widened. It was absurd that he didn't know what his own smile looked like.

Joy shot through him, accompanied by another easily deflected surge. The truth was irrefutable. Everything changed in that moment. His future rewritten. "You're right. This is love. I love you." Such simple words. Words he'd *known* he would never utter.

Her smile was a thing of radiant beauty. "I think the soup can wait. I need you in me. Need that connection to you that will never stop."

He cleared his throat as he pulled her closer. "I'm afraid my limited experience as left me a rather inexperienced lover. I want to learn what pleases you."

She pressed her finger over his mouth. "You did just fine before. And together we'll discover how to please each other." She playfully bit at his lower lip. "So many things to explore."

They left a trail of clothes as they made their way to the bedroom.

Splotches of color danced across his vision as he sealed the door.

"Do you see that?" She waved the air in front of her.

"Physical manifestation of our individual psi. Psi that will become one."

She took his hand and led him to the still-rumpled bed. Yet another ordinary scene in a normal life, but one completely new to him.

He guided her onto her back, and she spread her legs and squirmed with anticipation. The light under her skin was mesmerizing. Undulating and beautiful.

Her sex was closely trimmed. He trailed his fingers over her core, and her responsive moan had his cock pulsing. He stroked her wet, slick folds. The sounds she made worked him like nothing else.

The thought of her doing that with him buried deep was nearly too much.

"Armond."

He knew what she wanted. Knew what they both needed. He cursed himself for not believing sooner. For not studying the art of lovemaking. "I swear, I am going to spend my days learning how to please you in an infinite number of ways."

"I'm glad to hear that, but this can't wait."

Their psi had become entwined like rope, and undulated in an increasing tempo. He placed himself at her entrance and she pulled him in.

She gripped him with quivering muscles as he began moving his hips.

Their psi pulsed, and he growled out at the pleasure that

radiated through him. Them. This wasn't him alone. Never again.

Colors of blue and amber flashed across his vision.

"It's getting hard to see." Even as she spoke, her body matched his rhythm, her need fueling his own fire.

"We're merging." Tension rose; it was impossibly good. Too good. Too right. Faster, his body had a mind of its own as his scrotum tightened and the orgasm exploded.

Colors burst, and they moved into another plane. Awareness of the physical evaporating.

"Where are we?" Her voice echoed in his head.

"This is us. Our essence. That which we are beyond our bodies."

"It's beautiful."

It was. They were a part of something. Gossamer strands of stunning colors existed everywhere and nowhere. They *were* the strands and pulses of light. A web of infinite possibilities stretched in all directions. They were here and there all at once.

Reality returned in a heartbeat. He lay atop her, his forehead pressed to hers, heartbeats slowing to normal.

She peppered kisses on his lips, cheeks and chin. "That was...incredible."

"There's another thing that happens with psi-mates," Armond said.

"What's that?"

"We can communicate telepathically."

"But how...*do I do this?"* Her eyes widened on a grin. *"This is so cool!"* The way her body squirmed in her excitement sent pulses of pleasure to his core.

"There are distance limitations," he toyed with a silky strand of her hair. "but it could come in handy with the competition."

The happiness that flowed between them was a force of its own. A beautiful thing. Solid. Energized. Perfect.

SABINE PRIESTLEY

"I never thought I'd end up with someone like you," Vin said. "I always figured it would be a more...well-rounded man. Someone who shared my love of food."

His laugh came from the heart, and was the oddest thing he'd ever heard. "I never expected to be with anyone, but if I had, you would not have been it either. Don't misunderstand, I love your body, every curve you have is a wonder. It's your exuberance, your talking, I would not have guessed."

"My love of life can be hard to take at times."

He caressed her, reveling in her silky skin. "You saved me from a solitary existence."

Her love, and her sadness at his past, flowed across their bond. "I bet this bumps our ratings. They're going to want to watch."

"I am not having my first days or weeks of real sex broadcast to the galaxy."

"Might be fun to look back on when we're old and wrinkly."

"I think not." He gently slid out of her, and she curled into his side.

"Your smile is transformative, Armond. And that laugh? I hope to hear a lot more of that."

"With you at my side, I suspect you will not be disappointed."

Her stomach growled, and she giggled. "It's time for that soup."

CHAPTER 7

*A*s they approached the outlander territory, Armond experienced a strong sense of déjà vu. The constellation was the same as it was in their galaxy, which made no sense whatsoever. How could two galaxies have overlapping star systems? Then again, as vast as the universe was, everything was statically possible, as improbable as it may seem. This had to be the perfect example.

Marty wasn't wrong in the patrols the outlanders enforced. They were currently docked at Vortran. It was the last populated planet on the fringe of outlander space, and allowed them to monitor the activity without drawing attention. Interestingly, in this precise location in his galaxy was a planet called Vantor. They had nearly identical letters. Another coincidence?

He and Vin stood examining the holographic map of their destination.

"How are we going to get into that? We can't just fly in," Vin said. "Where do we start?"

"An exact location will be provided upon your successful arrival on Setara Blue."

"Figures," Vin said. "Okay, how about we hitch a ride? We can take a job on board a freighter going in."

"That's doable, but how will we get back out? I can only assume we will make our presence known when we obtain the next clue."

"Steal a ship?" Vin said.

"What if there aren't any?" Armond countered. "What we could really use right now is a couple of my distorters. I could simply open a portal and get it."

"A portal will be available on the planet's surface." Marty sat in a jump seat against the bulkhead.

Nothing and no one pissed off Armond more than that damnable AI. "You could have shared that with us on Omagar instead of nearly killing us."

"You didn't ask."

Vin grabbed his arm before he lost his temper.

"Feeds are live. If you're going to get angry, make it flashy. But try not to damage the console."

Armond turned his focus to the jump seat and it transmuted in a visually impressive manner, leaving behind a steaming ball of unrecognizable substance. "I could do that to you next," he said to Marty, who remained seated on air.

A crackling sound emitted from the speakers, but nothing else.

Armond's silent laughter rippled through their bond and into Vin.

"The viewers are going to love that. Well done. Feel better?"

"Oddly, yes."

"Welcome to humanity."

IT TOOK TWO DAYS, BUT THEY FINALLY SECURED POSITIONS aboard a freighter going into outlander territory. As far as Armond could determine, Setara Blue was the only destination within the space that non-outlanders could travel to, even as working crew. That in itself was interesting. Probably why it was selected as the repository of the next objective - the contest organizers had to get to it as well. Then again, if they had the ability to create portals in the same fashion he did with the distorters back in his galaxy, there were no limits. Except this outlander business was fishy. Time would tell. Time.

He thought again about his trip to Sigma Vector 9 to assist Marco Dar and his future mate Zara. They'd said he'd met his mate. That much had come true, and now they were headed into outlander territory.

And they were planning on using a portal. Interesting.

The three-day trip was a pain in the ass. Crew quarters were nothing more than bunk beds with no privacy. Intimacy, a key factor for newly-bonded psi-mates, was nonexistent, and they both suffered. The ship's air was cold, and stank of inefficient scrubbers.

When they approached the spaceport, reality did another flip. This wasn't Setara Blue, as they called it here. He knew it as Sigma Vector 9. The downtrodden dump they'd gone to in order to retrieve Marco's sentient AI com unit.

So, was it the same space present in two galaxies, or an alternate reality? Could he simply take Vin and leave? He seriously doubted that. Everything surrounding the system was foreign. Somehow this place overlapped, but how? Could this region exist in multiple bubble verses? Armond had no idea how to prove or disprove any of the theories occupying his attention.

"You ready?" Vin's voice brought him back to the present.

Whether or not they were in his galaxy, they had to finish the contest. One thing was for certain: the Corporation would never let him into a place he could escape from. Not intentionally, at least. Did they even know this existed in the Milky Way? "Ready."

"They have us on the ship's manifesto for the return trip in two days."

Neither of them expected to be on board.

"Marty, how do we activate the portal?" Armond asked.

"Simply enter '1618' into your com and I will bring you back."

"Understood."

The trip to the planet surface was on a skiff that looked to be on the verge of disintegration. It had seen better days and wasn't going to see many more. The other passengers were mostly crew like themselves, heading out for some PTO. The groundside spaceport was typical for shipping hubs. Bustling with activity and more functional than ascetically appealing.

Armond tapped his earpiece. "You with us. Marty?"

"Affirmative."

"Well? Where are we going?" Vin asked.

"Sending your destination now."

The coordinates popped up on his com. It was a large warehouse on the outskirts of town. A tingle ran down his spine. He'd never been there, but knew exactly what it would look like thanks to Marco's description. Was the corporation playing into this on purpose, or was it more entanglement?

"What's wrong?" Vin asked, running her palm down his arm.

"Let's get a transport and I'll explain."

They followed transportation symbols outside the ground terminal. The air was hot and humid, but the sun shone in the afternoon sky.

They picked up an open-air automated hovercraft that was about as comforting as the skiff they'd taken down. He wouldn't want to see the surface of the seats under a black light.

"So, what's going on?" Vin asked again.

"Three months ago I was on assignment with a fellow Earth Protector, Marco Dar. We had to retrieve a com unit."

"And?"

"It was located in a warehouse on the edge of town. This town, on this planet."

"But you said this wasn't your galaxy."

"It's not."

"Then how?"

"I have no idea, but I believe you're going to meet Marco and his mate Zara before this is over. Or, more correctly in this time-line, his future mate."

She tilted her head in the way she did. "I'm going to your galaxy? Which is here. That makes no sense whatsoever."

"Indeed."

"But, if we're in your space, doesn't that mean we can get you home?"

"I'm fairly certain the Corporation would never let that happen. Unless they don't know, which is possible. This system is the same as in my galaxy, but nothing surrounding it is. I think it best we stay focused on our completion." He took her hand in his and interlaced their fingers. Such a simple thing to do, but for him it was profound.

The vehicle pulled to a stop in the unpaved parking lot of the warehouse. The sun was setting, and a few other vehicles were arriving, mostly dropping off. This was a happening place, apparently.

"We're here, Marty. Any further clues?"

"The center of attention is what you need. Take that which has all eyes and don't get caught, or all this work will have been for naught." Marty spoke in a highly inflected mysterious voice.

"As usual, not very helpful," Vin said.

"I do my best," the AI replied.

"You're right, Armond. He's an asshole." Vin gave his hand a squeeze and winked.

"The irony is not lost on me, given that I do not have said orifice," Marty replied.

They made their way inside behind a group of scantily-clad women being tailed by some beefy tattooed men. Whether they were there for protection or participation wasn't clear. The rhythmic beat of music got increasingly louder as they went deeper into the structure. Thirty feet in, and the ceiling opened up. Four stories, all open in the center. Each floor appeared to have a different vibe going. An elevator stood against the back wall, and stairs were scattered seemingly randomly from floor to floor.

"Don't hate me," Vin said, leaning in close enough to be heard, "but this looks like fun."

A few weeks ago, he would have disagreed without another thought, but now? Perhaps, under different circumstances. Fun was a foreign concept. He could think of no one better to explore it with than the blue skinned, stereo-voiced woman next to him.

"Where do we start?" Vin asked.

He scanned the layout again. "I suggest we hit the top floor and work our way down."

Being as it was still relatively early, it wasn't overly crowded. Heading toward the lift, they passed a crew that was busy setting up for something on a stage against the back wall.

He used his psi to summon the elevator. They stepped onto a familiar-looking platform. One with seemingly no walls.

"This is the elevator?" Vin gripped his arm tightly.

"It's perfectly safe. Here." He took her hand and extended it outward until it came into contact with an invisible resistance. "We use this technology on my homeworld of Sandaria."

"Good thing this building is only four floors. I'd be taking the stairs otherwise." She closed her eyes and pressed her face to his chest as they rode up. He breathed in her floral scent; there was nothing he wouldn't do for this woman.

The upper level was quiet, only tables and various seating arrangements. Half of the floor was cordoned off as private offices, each having a glass wall that overlooked the venue.

They stood on the far side of the offices, and Armond was about to turn when a man inside caught his eye. A bald man. Large and well-built. He had a scar on the side of his face and a tattoo above it, on his head. He fit the description of the outlander that had tangled with Marco.

Vin followed his gaze. "He's hot."

Armond sent a pulse of pleasure across their bond. "He'll never do that for you."

She flashed him a wicked smile and her left nipple. "Damn straight."

Completely his opposite, she was perfect for him.

He turned back to find the outlander watching them. The fact he'd seen Vin's breast made him both angry and proud. The man would never touch his woman.

The outlander smirked and gave a nod of appreciation. Behind him in the office, an interior door opened. Three people exited a room. Framed by the doorway was something he'd never expected to see again. It was a monolith, just like the one that had been stolen from the Portal Masters on Sandaria and ultimately stored on Earth when the Cavacent Clan fled the crumbling empire.

His recognition must have showed, as the outlander's expression was now one of intense interest.

The implications were staggering.

"*Armond, I saw that before,*" Vin said. "*When you healed me. During your initiation.*"

When the Portal Masters died. She squeezed his hand.

"*I doubt it's the same one.*" Unless the temporal anomaly had completely change the timeline. "*I think I figured out how this region exists in two galaxies at once.*" He pulled his attention back to Vin.

"*Where's it come from?*" she asked.

"*We don't know. An alien communicated through it with a fellow Earth Protector and his mate. Their guess was that the society was far advanced from ours. It is a mystery for another day, but worth noting.*" Armond took her arm and steered her back toward the elevator. "Come on. Let's keep searching."

There was nothing unusual on the third floor. Another bar, a dance area.

Behind them, the outlander and three others descended to the ground level. The bald one watched him intensely.

A moment later, the volume increased from below, and cheers went up from a growing crowd. "Looks like we may have found our mark."

They headed for the lift. The venue may look like a dump on the outside, but they'd spared no expense on the interior.

Vin stood with her face pressed against his back. "*I feel like I'm going to fall off the edge.*"

"*We're almost down.*"

The doors slid open, and they faced the stage. Sitting on a stone pillar behind and to the right of a slender woman wearing a full-body jumpsuit, was a box very much like the others. There appeared to be some sort of contest going on, and that box was the prize to be awarded at the end of the night.

"*We could always enter. Maybe get lucky?*" Vin grinned. They both knew that wasn't going to happen.

"All we have to do is get our hands on it and port out." Armond said. "Marty, you there?"

"Of course. Anxiously awaiting your orders with rapt attention and pleasure."

Armond rolled his eyes. It had been about the extent of emotional display he allowed before. Now he had a much greater and far more satisfying realm from which to draw. "Can I just speak the numbers?"

"Negative. You must enter them on your com."

Senseless, but typical for the game show. "How long will it take you to activate the portal once I give the signal?"

"Nearly instantaneous, as I said before."

"You have a way of being somewhat misleading," Vin said.

"Surely you jest."

Armond caught sight of the outlander on the far side of the stage. "We've got company." Standing next to him were Ax and his new partner, Kayana, her red skin giving her a decidedly devilish appearance; but that may not have relevance in this galaxy.

"Shit," Vin said. "Should we make a run for it? Catch them off guard before the crowd gets too thick?"

The outlander handed them something, all the while looking straight at Armond.

"Let's see how close we can get to the stairs before we make our move." For the first time since meeting her, he feared her ample size might slow her down.

Everyone's attention was on that box and the speaker going on about its contents.

"They're moving," Vin said. "Run." She bolted at a speed that seemed impossible.

It took Armond a full second to process and follow after her.

Both teams were shoving their way through the crowd and onto the stage.

The outlander stood with his arms crossed and a smile plastered across his face.

Vin made it first and grabbed the box, but it wasn't budging. She leaned back and yelled for Armond.

He lunged forward, and four sets of hands collided on the pillar.

Ax smiled. "Orion says hello." He opened his palm on the box, and everything blinked out.

They were in a portal. A longer than usual portal. But not long enough. The next instant, they stood in the galley of *No Commitments*.

Zara had just landed on top of Marco, both of them piled on the remains of the shattered dining table.

"WhooHoo! What a fucking ride that was!" Marco cupped Zara's face with both hands and planted a kiss on her lips.

Zara's shock was obvious as she pushed herself up to sitting.

"Sorry, darling." He gripped her upper arms. "I almost died just now. Kind of glad to be here."

ZARA SCRAMBLED TO HER FEET. "ARE YOU OK?"

"Oh, baby you have no idea. I was running for my life back there, then you just popped right in front of me." He rolled over and stood facing Armond and Vin. "Dude, what happened? And who's this?"

Armond shook his head, disoriented. He hadn't been sure how this would play out. If it would play out. Even after meeting Vin, Marco and Zara's tale had seemed far-fetched. No denying it now. He had no memory of this next interaction, only that which Marco had told him. The part he remembered, they wouldn't be here for, having already left. In theory. Fascinating.

Marco gave them a puzzled look and turned back to Zara. "I just kissed you, right? I'm not hallucinating this?"

"Yes, you just kissed me. When that thing beeped, Armond touched it and disappeared. Scared me half to death."

Marco shot him a furious look. "You left her? Where the hell did you go?"

"It appears the question isn't where, but when." He wondered how much parallel there would be between his interaction with Marco and Zara now, and that which had occurred three months ago. Three months for him. Not for them.

Vin held fast to his arm. "I take it these are the friends you mentioned? From your past?"

Armond nodded. *"My past, their present."*

"Armond, when did you change your clothes, and who is this?" Marco motioned to Vin.

Vin squeezed his arm. *"I can't understand a word he says."*

"The translators must need bidirectional feedback. He's speaking my native language."

"Sounds better on you."

He smiled at her. Marco and Zara had both said his behavior had been different. *He* still wasn't used to the fact that he could spontaneously smile. It had to be extremely odd for them.

"What the hells is going on here?" Marco stared at him, then looked at Zara. He kissed her again.

Zara gave in momentarily, then shoved him back. "What do you think you're doing?"

Of course, in this timeline, they weren't bonded yet; and Ru hadn't transformed.

"Reality Check," Marco said. "I figure I must be hallucinating. None of this makes any sense."

"Did we make it?" Ru's familiar voice emanated from Marco's pocket.

"Dude, almost forgot you." Marco withdrew the com.

"You made it," Zara said smiling. "But we've got a little situation here."

"A situation indeed," Armond said. "Where are we?" He knew, of course.

"Don't you think we should get out of here before chatting?" Zara asked. "You know, outlanders and all."

Armond smiled again, drawing another perplexed look from Marco.

"You're really enjoying this, aren't you?" Vin asked.

"Tremendously." The problem was, he wasn't sure of the protocol. Should he go along with some facsimile of what he knew had transpired before? He knew some pretty key elements regarding their lives. Like the fact that they were now psi-mates, for one. But what if that changed something? What if the revelation caused Zara, or more likely Marco, to alter their future? The future he had just come from. No. Best not to disturb that. He'd follow what Marco and Zara had said.

Marco turned to go to the bridge, but paused. "Do you know what ship you're on?"

"This is the *No Commitments.*" For now. "She's a Delta class transport. One of twenty-three currently owned and operated by the Cavacent Clan, the head of which is Lord Rucon Cavacent, who was responsible for naming the vessel that is primarily yours."

Regardless of the time loop, he did have to convince Marco he was Armond.

"And what's our current passcode?"

Armond nearly responded with the code from three months ago, but that's not what he would have done if he hadn't known. "Snow White." The pass from his now.

Marco scratched his jaw. "What's the date? Earth date, relative."

This one he knew. Weird day, for sure. "March 19, 2018."

"Dude, that's three months from now."

Yes it was. "It appears we have arrived from the future. Perhaps a distortion encountered during our jump." They'd told him he'd said something like that.

Apparently satisfied, Marco left for the bridge.

"Come," Zara said. "Have a seat." She pointed to the table, and set about making a pot of tea.

They chatted until Marco returned and wrapped up quickly. He could only hope they hadn't changed anything.

"What if we just stay?" Vin asked.

"I considered it. But that's not the way it played out before. I don't want to change anything. Or do anything different."

"Makes sense. Strange as all this is."

"One way other another, we have to win this race."

"Yes, but we're going back empty-handed."

～

ARMOND RETRIEVED HIS COM AND PAUSED BEFORE ENTERING the code. 1618. Was the sequence coincidence or intentional? Perhaps it was one of the subplots that was going to run through the season. A hidden thread to be discovered sooner or later. He entered the digits.

The familiar pull of a portal enveloped them, along with an unexpected aroma of cinnamon. A moment later, they stood in space.

Vin latched onto his arm and looked around wildly. "We seem to be missing a ship. And why am I suddenly so turned on?"

It was warm as Armond breathed in a lungful. "We have air."

His mate was right. Their psi was pulsating with sexual tension.

"Smells like *bloorana*," Vin said.

"I know it as cinnamon." They stood on an invisible platform, and a stunning nebula lay before them. "It's beautiful," Vin said. *"I seriously want you inside me right now."*

Before Armond could reply, an omnidirectional voice spoke.

"I hoped you would appreciate the view." Spoken in a deep male timbre.

"Orion?" Armond asked.

"Correct."

Vin's curiosity pinged. "Care to fill me in?" Her amusement rippled across their bond, along with a mental image of him pounding into her.

"When the reign of Portal Masters fell in the Sandarian Empire, Orion communicated with Balastar and Kit through a monolith like the one we saw on Setara Blue. He called it the Gateway Keeper. His energy has an amplifying effect on our bond."

Vin shot a burst of pleasure at him. "I'll say."

"Behave." He stroked her cheek. "Orion assisted us in securing a place to keep the device safe. What are we doing here, Orion?"

"Your psi signature was detected when you used the portal. It was an anomaly. The only humanoids allowed to use this inter-galactic portal are of the outlanders, and they do not possess your form of psi. Is everything stable on Earth? With the Gateway Keeper?"

"As far as I know, it is where we left it."

"That is well."

"Are you responsible for the time distortion?"

"Yes. It was necessary in order for us to have a discussion. The outlander Varian assisted me." Orion's foreign psi buzzed through him. And Vin too, judging by her response. It felt good.

"You are newly-bonded?" Orion asked.

"We are," Armond said.

The entity had been mesmerized with Balastar and Kit's bond as well. Was it because of the pleasure inherent in such a tie?

"This is my mate, Vin." Armond looped his fingers through hers.

"Greetings, Vin."

"Hello." She waved a hand, but there was no object to focus upon.

"Orion," Armond continued, fascinated. "Are you also responsible for the outlander territories existing in both galaxies?"

"Not me personally, but one of my kind is. As with myself in your galaxy, that entity plays in this space. They are aware of my involvement in your home star system, and notified me of your presence here. It is fortunate, because you would have remained terminated otherwise."

"Remained terminated?" Vin said.

"Because Armond was not cleared by the outlanders, he was terminated during the attempt to use a portal back to your *Galaxy Riders* ship. Hence my need to create the temporal distortion."

That was going to take some time to process. "Why the *No Commitments*?"

"That was an error on my part. Having the outlanders exist in dual space presents certain complications with portal theory."

Advanced tech, but not infallible. "Will you allow us to travel between these galaxies like the outlanders?"

There was a puff of air, and the smell of cinnamon increased. Their psi buzzed with sensual energy.

"There's an interesting play of emotion going on with Orion." Vin spoke over their bond. *"He's talking to someone else."*

"What are they saying?"

"Can't tell exactly. An argument, but good-natured."

"The entity that has precedence in the dual existence of outlander territory will allow such travel, but you must win the Octiron race first. She is what you would call, a fan."

"And if we lose?" Vin's fear was strong across their bond.

"I will see Armond is safely returned to his galaxy, but you, Vin, will remain in yours."

"That is not happening." Vin's voice belied her anxiety.

"My apologies," Orion said. "I was only notified of Armond's presence in the first place out of courtesy. I can make no demands in this situation. But, due to my relationship with the Cavacent Clan whom Armond works for, I will ensure his safety."

"In that case," Armond said, "we need to return."

"Certainly," Orion said. "Please send my greetings to Lord Cavacent, and of course Balastar and Kit. Tell them I will visit soon. And now, I will return you to your original destination. Is that your wish?"

"Yes."

"Farewell, Armond and Vin."

A MOMENT LATER, THEY WERE BACK ON THE BRIDGE OF GALAXY *Riders.*

Vin took Armond's hand. She needed his touch. Needed to know he was here. The thought of being separated from him had a vice grip on her heart, and had totally messed with the sexual buzz they'd had going.

"Welcome home," Marty said. He wore a strange get-up of pointy leather shoes, a thin brimmed hat, and puffed on a long, skinny inhaler. "You do not appear to have the box. Am

I to assume you failed?" He blew an odorless cloud in their faces.

The lights on the infernal vidbots lit up like Trinanthian spark-bugs in summer.

"A temporary setback," Armond said.

"They cheated," Vin said, exaggerating her displeasure for the feed. "The alien entity helped them. What's next, Marty. We need to get moving."

"Your next destination is a most impressive anomaly." Marty flicked his hand, and a hologram appeared.

"What is that?" She panned out and did a 360-degree rotation. Confused, she superimposed a scale along the vertical and horizontal. "Sweet mother. It's enormous."

What looked like a mountain rose slightly over a mile high: 1.005 miles to be exact. She did a quick scan; the closest star system wasn't too far at just under .7 light years.

Nothing on the surface of the object appeared to be man-made. No indication of engines, lights, or anything to hint of sentience. "Marty, any readings? Is it an asteroid?"

"I can locate no sensors within range of the object. Visual analysis provides no clues as to its composition. We need to get closer."

"How long will it take?"

"Just over twenty-seven hours."

"Get us moving."

Armond waited for the confirmation, then led her to the bedroom. The sensations pouring into her were a heady mix of love and lust. Need and aggressive desire matched by her own. There was no need for words, and they discarded their clothes and physically calmed the turmoil within. The man may be inexperienced, but he made her body sing. They couldn't be separated. She wouldn't allow it. She'd spend the rest of her life hunting for him if she had to, because there wasn't another being in the universe that could take his place.

Nearly twenty hours and multiple orgasms later, they were curled up on the couch in front of the VR fireplace. "I have a feeling this may be it." Vin said, sipping a deep, rich red wine.

"I sense it as well. We're not going to be alone on, or in, that mountain. Space Mountain."

"Space Mountain?" Vin asked.

"There's an amusement park on Earth. It's a thrill ride. A cart attached to metal rails that travels relatively fast for terrestrials. They call it Space Mountain."

"Seems appropriate."

Two hours out, Marty started reporting data on the anomaly. As suspected, they weren't the only ones heading toward it. Three other ships were converging upon the structure. Interestingly, they all had different interception points. They may be in there together, but they were going at it alone, at least to start with.

Vin couldn't contain her energy. She paced. Bonding with Armond had altered something fundamental within her. She had more energy, and was more focused than ever before. And now losing wasn't an option. She suspected a significant part of her desire originated with Armond, but it was her now, too.

Once they had the object on screens, it was difficult to take her eyes off it. The substance was a black metallic material, but the surface was indeed more like that of a natural formation than anything manufactured. Protruding rock formations and deep crevices covered the thing from base to tip.

They were slowly approaching when Marty pinged with

more information. "Two degrees to our left we will find a docking bay. Of sorts. We are to engage the airlocks and board from here. You may select from the equipment presently available in the airlock lockers."

A quick check left them with the breather helmets. They had enough oxygen for five hours each. Wouldn't do much if the place was depressurized, but there wasn't anything they could do about that.

"Marty, any idea where the others are docking?" Vin asked.

"They are also approaching their perspective entry points."

"Do we know where those locations are?" Vin tried again, and donned her collar.

"I am privy to that knowledge."

"And we are not?" Armond asked, his anger spiking.

"Correct."

The now empty locker went the way of the jump seat on the bridge and lay in a smoldering heap.

"I find the outbursts oddly therapeutic," Armond said, a little louder than necessary for the benefit of the vidbot.

"Not surprising, given that you've had to contain your emotions most of your life." Vin sent a wave of love across their bond.

"I keep thinking about how it would feel if I did that to Marty." Armond gave her a barely perceptible wink.

"Very funny," Marty said. "I thought you'd like to know, there are an additional four ships approaching."

"Looks like it could get interesting," Armond said.

"One of them is team *Starry Night*." Marty leaned against the airlock hatch, wearing hiking gear and boots.

"Haven't run into them since the opening," Vin said.

"Pick up anything useful about them?" Armond asked.

"Mia's a force, and I believe she's honorable. D'Arek is privileged, cold, and proud. They may not know it yet, but he'd kill to protect her. Maybe we can use that to our advantage."

Marty was right when he said it was a docking bay of sorts. There was no support, only the coupling rings for the airlock. "Once we're inside, I want you to decouple, Marty." Armond said. "Stay at this relative location in case we lose contact."

"What are you thinking?" Vin asked.

"If this thing decides to accelerate, our umbilical cord will be ripped out." Armond fastened his own collar.

"Good point." Vin ran an atmosphere check as soon as the access chamber was pressurized. "Air pressure, temperature, and oxygen are all nominal."

"Gravity?" Armond asked.

"There is indeed gravity," Marty said.

She pressed the panel, and the doors slid open. There was a sweet scent. Something familiar, but elusive. "I know that smell, but I can't place it."

"Reminiscent of something edible." Armond used his psi to close the hatch behind them.

The window to the interior of the mountain showed a long, smooth corridor that dead-ended a hundred feet or so ahead. Passages led off to the left and right.

"Time to play." As they stepped into the corridor, they were slammed into the wall, Vin landing partially on top of Armond. She choked back a laugh. "He wasn't wrong when he said we have gravity."

"No doubt he oriented the ship incorrectly on purpose." Armond's annoyance filtered through their bond.

Marty remained silent as they got to their feet.

A moment later, the AI disengaged the ship as instructed.

"When do we get more specific details, Marty?" Vin asked.

"When I provide you with them, of course."

Armond was a step ahead of her when they reached the T-junction at the end of the hall.

It caught them both by surprise when he fell. Straight up.

"Stop," Armond said, a few feet from the ceiling.

"What's happening?" Vin didn't move, but craned her neck to see Armond.

He was getting to his feet. On the ceiling. "At least my psi is fully functional within this structure."

"Glad that was you and not me. Could have broken my neck."

Armond's psi wrapped around her and pulled her forward, rotating her position relative to him as he set her down.

"That's seriously disorienting." Vin's stomach lurched as she dealt with the mental fear of falling from what was the ceiling a moment before.

The corridor on either side appeared to be identical to the one they'd just left, with pathways leading left and right.

"Which way do we go?" Vin asked.

There was a hint of air movement flowing through the halls.

"Doesn't matter until we get an objective and need to know where we're at."

Vin took out her com and activated the laser. She etched two arrows on the corner of the wall. "First arrow is the direction of gravity. The second is the direction we take." She then snapped an image of the arrows and made notes. "We do this right and we should be able to sort out generally where we are."

They made steady progress, marking their trajectory. The gravitational orientation changed at nearly every intersection. By the eighth turn, she was totally lost, even with her notes.

They were eleven turns in when the lights went out. Total darkness engulfed them. And then they fell.

Armond grabbed her and enveloped them in a psi cocoon. Gravity played a wicked game as they were pushed and pulled, not only up and down but left and right.

They came to a stop and the lights re-engaged.

They were at a forty-five degree angle a few feet above a metallic floor in a seriously massive chamber.

Armond righted their relative position and set them down.

Being enveloped in Armond's psi felt pretty damn amazing, even when it wasn't a sexual thing.

The open space spanned hundreds of yards deep as well as high. Dozens of passageways led out in all directions, and a dizzying array of staircases connected them, each oriented differently, from a gravitational perspective.

Other teams were spotted around the massive juncture.

A warm sweet wind blew strands of hair across her face.

"Look!" Vin pointed to the far ceiling.

Mia Jag and D'Arek had just tumbled out of a passage far above. They nearly went over, which would have put them in a precarious position gravity wise, possibly going airborne and falling. With the agility of her feline genes, Mia leapt to the safety of the passageway above. D'Arek followed behind.

"What are they doing?" Vin asked.

"They appear to be fastening a rope," Armond replied.

"Be careful," Vin called out. "It's farther than it looks, and there's no telling what the gravity will do in the middle."

"Are you helping them?" Armond asked.

Vin crossed her arms. "Something is going on. It's the right thing to do. Don't know why."

D'Arek was descending on the rope with impressive speed.

There was a tremble in the mountain. A feeling of fore-boding settled upon her.

Above, D'Arek was nearly down when a stronger tremor hit. The rope swung in a gravity defying, jerky pattern. He dropped to the floor in a crouch and looked up. "Mia—Now!"

With feline grace, she griped the rope and launched over the edge. Halfway down she careened wildly. D'Arek struggled to steady her, but gravity was wreaking havoc.

"Help her," Vin said, the command shooting down their bond.

Armond didn't even blink, simply reached out with his psi, caught Mia, and steadied her descent. She landed in D'Arek's arms a moment later.

Vin nodded at Mia and turned to Armond. "They owe us one."

"We do not know they will see it that way."

"Mia will. Trust me." She loved being able to caress him over their bond.

"Are you enjoying yourselves?" Marty's voice came over their coms. "The Corporation is live streaming, and your ratings just shot up three percent."

Vin snorted.

"I can now tell you: your objective is at the top of the mountain, that being the narrowest section. All teams are being notified simultaneously."

She locked eyes with Armond. Her notes were useless. "Which way is up?"

CHAPTER 8

The other teams were either eyeing the cavern or exiting through the closest passage. It was a bizarre sight, having people sticking to walls and the ceiling. It would be a fun place to explore in other circumstances. "We can't go till we know which way is up," Vin said. "Marty, which way?"

"I suggest you go left. Or perhaps right. On the other hand, down might be up."

"Bite me." Vin turned to Armond. "So what do we do? We can't just guess."

"No, but we have an advantage." Armond stroked her cheek.

"How so?"

"*My psi is fully functional. 'Up' is either to our right or left. The other direction is narrower. We're going to have to traverse a way before I can tell if the width is increasing or decreasing.*"

"Left it is, then," Vin said, with a feeling that things were finally sorting out.

"Why left?"

"We have a fifty percent chance of being right, and limited time. Let's go."

They'd been going at a decent clip for just shy of four minutes before Armond let her know she was wrong.

"Seriously?" Vin snapped. "Why is it every time I have a fifty-fifty shot at something, I get it wrong ninety-five percent of the time?"

They turned back the way they'd come and picked up the pace again.

"I'm only incorrect eighty percent of the time," Armond said. "Next time, I'll choose."

"Fine by me, but you just jinxed it."

They reached the second gravity shift and Armond enveloped them in his psi and oriented them with the new down as indicated by her etching. The moment he released her, they both slammed into the wall next to them.

Vin stood, rubbing her bruised elbow. "I take it down is now sideways again."

"Apparently," Armond said, standing and reaching out a hand to help her up.

Vin staggered slightly when they moved forward. It was one thing to have gravity telling you which way was up, but another to convince your mind of the same.

It was slow going with multiple gravity shifts, but they finally made it back to the central cavern. Inevitably, the direction they needed to go in was now straight up.

Vin eyed the passage above. "Can you get us up there?"

"Too far." Armond quickly scanned the lattice of stairways. "This way."

They started up a stone staircase that protruded from the wall. It was a good five feet deep, but with no rail, Vin stayed close to the inside. They were three quarters of the way up when gravity began shifting again.

Armond grabbed her arm, and they waited a few heartbeats. "We're moving perpendicular."

They both crouched, hands on the steps. "The bottom of the steps will be the top," Armond said.

They crab-walked their way to the edge of the spine and over. Vertigo hit hard, along with panic.

"You're fine, Vin." Armond sent calm and a burst of pleasure across their bond.

She closed her eyes and continued their crouched movement until they stood firmly on the wall that was previously next to and below them.

Armond helped her stand, and wrapped his arms around her.

"I have to get out of this cavern," Vin said, fighting her fear and vertigo.

Armond kissed her, waking her passion and providing a much-needed diversion. "Better?"

His smile grounded her. "Yes."

"We're almost there." She stayed between the wall and Armond, and they made it to their target passage.

Relief washed over her as they stepped inside. "Hope I never have to do that again."

The passage was upside down from their original orientation, but that was fine, as they were moving in the right direction now.

"Some of the teams are getting closer to the objective," Marty piped in cheerily.

"Are we one of them?" Vin asked.

"Perhaps. Perhaps, not."

A bolt of anger shot from Armond. With no target, a section of the wall to their left morphed into an odd-looking patch like puckered leather. At the same time, the floor lurched, and sent them both tumbling forward.

"Marty, what just happened?" Vin asked.

"The structure you are in has begun acceleration. One moment... Three of our competitors have been disqualified due to the fact their ships docking bays are now disabled."

"Ha!" Vin pumped the air with her fist. "Thank you, Armond."

"Any of those teams ahead of us?" Armond asked.

"One. Possibly more," Marty replied.

"Why do we even bother with him?" Vin said.

They made their way as quickly as possible. They were traversing a particularly long passage when a gravity shift occurred, slamming them both against the wall.

"Damn it!" Same shoulder as before. "I'm going to be green."

"Green?" Armond stood and held out a hand to her.

"I turn green when I bruise." She took the assist.

"All of you?"

"No. That's a stupid question. Just here," she motioned to her shoulder. "Where I've hit the wall twice now."

"Technically you hit the floor. Twice."

Vin growled at him, and pink ripples inked across her skin.

"So, this is you angry." Armond stroked her arm, following the delicate pink traces.

They vanished instantly under his touch.

"I'm learning a lot about you today." Love and deeply textured emotion flowed across their bond. "I look forward to learning more."

Vin leaned in and pressed her lips to his. It was a teaser, and far too short.

"Let's figure out how to win this thing." She didn't want to think about what would happen if they lost.

"Agreed."

They made quick time after that, and rounded the last corner. At the end of the corridor was door that appeared to open into space. As they approached, they heard footfalls. And D'Arek's deep voice.

"Run!" They bolted through the door and slammed into the wall, which was now the floor.

"I'm so tired of this shit!" Vin screamed, getting to her feet.

Across the chamber, Mia burst through another door with D'Arek on her heels. They had luck on their side, or help, as the floor was still the floor for them.

Between the two teams stood a clear podium, and mounted on the top was the Octiron prize box. And Mia was going to get it first.

Armond shot forward.

Not fast enough.

Mia snatched it up with a triumphant growl.

Vin came to a stop next to Armond.

"It can't end this way." She meant it. A life without him wasn't worth living. Not now.

"This is not the end."

A dangerous level of energy burst forth, and Armond seized Mia and D'Arek in a psi hold.

"What the hells are you doing?" D'Arek bellowed. "Release us, psi-freak, or you won't live to enjoy what you've stolen."

"Easy, everyone," Vin said. "We can all get out of this alive."

With Mia and D'Arek held together in Armond's psi, Vin had an unusually clear channel to their emotions. D'Arek was far more concerned for Mia's safety than the prize.

"Mia," Vin said. "If we don't win, Armond and I will be separated. Permanently."

D'Arek struggled with incredible force, but was unable to free himself. It only added to his mounting rage. "Don't listen to her, Mia. It's a trick—I've warned you to trust no one."

The energy streaming out of Armond was barely controlled, and increasing.

Vin shifted to deflect the energy, but the room had an unforeseen effect: instead of dissipating the force, it reflected it. Her muscles tensed as though hit by an electrical shock.

"Vin?" Armond's grip on the couple held, not realizing he was responsible for her distress. "What did you do to her?" He moved toward D'Arek.

"It was you, psi-freak. You're going to kill us all."

"Stop." Vin got the word out on inhale.

"Listen to her," Mia begged, her eyes wide with horror. "Both of you, stop arguing and Armond, just stop!"

"She's right," Vin gasped. "Armond, I can't deflect in here. You can't lose control." She managed another pain filled breath. "Mia, please—let us have it and we all live. He can't control his power. Not without me. And I can't do it in this room. We will all die here today if you don't."

"All right," Mia called. "Take the prize. You need it, we don't."

"Mia," D'Arek growled.

The Tygean gave him a pleading look. "D'Arek, please. Armond can't hold onto his power. The prize isn't worth our lives, or theirs."

"Either way, you lose," Vin managed.

"Wrong." Mia smiled at her partner. "Prize or no prize, either way, we win."

The Aurelian gave her a look of long-suffering, but then he nodded. "Very well. Armond, stand down. You have my word as an Aurelian that we will not try to prevent your winning."

"And my word as a Tygean," Mia added, placing the box on the podium and backing up.

"We won't forget this," Vin said. "Thank you."

The pair spun, and left them alone in the star-filled space.

"Looks like you managed to pull it off," Marty appeared next to them. He wore an over-the-top deep-blue formal get up that was covered in sequins. "I suggest you activate your breathers."

To their right, *Galaxy Riders* rose into view, it's airlock open and waiting.

They activated the collars, breathing the slightly metallic tasting air.

Vin took the box and they walked over to their ship. An odd pressure squeezed them as they passed from the platform into the airlock.

Armond closed the outer door, and they were back on board.

"We did it." The reality was sweeter than any delicacy Vin had ever tasted. The blue lines of her desire were writ large on her skin. "I am so turned on right now."

Armond laughed, and blasted her with his own desire. It was nearly enough to send her over the edge. "You store the box," he said. "I'll get us heading back to Primeara. I need to be inside you."

That didn't require a response. Vin headed for the galley and added the last prize to the cabinet with the others.

Armond met her in the hallway and backed her up against the bulkhead. He reached for her shirt and had it over her head in no time. Using his psi, he lifted her, removed her boots, socks and pants in seconds. The psi connection was intense and so damn good she rode an orgasm before he touched her again.

He set her down long enough to lose his clothes. Rock hard and pure perfection, he lifted her again and pinned her against the wall.

She sucked in a breath as the cool surface pressed against her back. Wrapping her legs around Armond, she savored the contrast of cold steel and the hard heat of the man before her.

"Are you ready for the rest of our lives?" He probed her slick entrance, teasingly. He had her pinned with his psi and every cell of her body was a pleasure point.

She hooked her ankles behind his back and pulled him home. A moan escaped her lips at the exquisite sensation. "I will always be ready for this. For you."

The only sound that followed was that of the sweet slapping as he pounded into her. She rode the tension as it built, the rising crescendo a manifestation of pure perfection.

He captured her cry of pleasure with a demanding kiss as he found his own release.

She held herself pressed against him as he pulsed inside and their heartbeats slowly returned to normal.

"Oh, bravo!" Marty stood behind them and clapped theatrically. "That was spectacular. And may I just say, you have the finest ass this side of Omega Prime."

Armond buried his face in her neck. *"I forgot the damn feeds."*

Vin laughed. *"Don't worry. I'm going to keep this one for our own use. Maybe make a few more to go with it after this fiasco is done. Besides, Marty's right."*

"This must never be seen in my galaxy. Marco Dar would be an even more insufferable ass."

Vin gently bit his neck and smiled into those clear blues. "We seem to be having an ass fixation."

His laughter was the perfect end to the perfect beginning.

BACK ON PRIMEARA, THEY WERE READY FOR THE FINAL ceremony. The weather was warm and breezy, the outside event hosted on a rooftop.

They stepped out of the transport provided by Octiron.

"Strange-looking building," Vin said. It was extremely tall, and decorated with oddly-placed geometric shapes.

"Reminds me of an architectural style on Earth called Art Deco," Armond said. "I'll show you soon."

They rode an external elevator to the top, which framed stunning views of the city. The rooftop was sublime. A cool breeze and clear sky provided the perfect setting, and the media was out in full force. There was also a generous spattering of previous contestants and winners.

The multi-colored orbs hovered above the gathering as they had during the pre-departure event. Vin wondered where she could purchase the lights. Smaller, of course, but they'd make a beautiful addition to any entertaining space.

Suede Harrington was in full swing, making the rounds and talking to contestants present and past. The media vidbots followed him in a swarm. He was in his element, and puffed up like a Trinathian cock surrounded by his females. In effect he was, with the blondes not far behind, chatting with anyone and everyone who came near.

A flash of blue light lit up the night sky in the distance. "What was that?" Armond asked.

"Probably an electrical storm," Vin said. "They're quite common here. Beautiful, but you don't want to be too close to one."

"We had similar phenomena on my home planet of Sandaria," Armond said. "They're seasonal, arriving every summer, with swirling purple and green clouds. Also potentially deadly."

"That sounds nice," Vin said. "Any chance of seeing it someday?"

"Sadly, not for another forty years."

"Why?"

A heavy feeling of sadness settled on their bond. "A portal

master named Gordat Prayda was driven to desperate measures during the fall of the Sandarian Empire. In an attempt to maintain control over the Gateway Keeper, he released a toxin on the planet. One which will remain for a fifty-year time span. Sandaria is under quarantine."

"Survivors?"

"Yes, but no way of extracting them safely. The toxin can survive space, and is extremely contagious. The survivors are living in bio-domes that were created using psi. An entire generation will know nothing but that existence."

"Wow. Hard to imagine."

After an eternally long fifteen minutes, Suede finally made his way to them. "And here we have our winning couple!"

Media vidbots swarmed around them, jostling into their assigned positions, creating a wall behind Suede. "And how are our lovebirds on this stellar evening?"

"Alive," Vin said.

Suede roared with laughter. "That is a fine thing, is it not, everyone?" He scanned the crowd that surrounded them, and the revelers joined in with jovial hollers. Mostly about Armond's back end.

"I wish he'd just get on with it so we could get it on." Vin placed her hand on the slight bulge in his pants. The crowd went wild.

Armond blasted her with an orgasm-producing wave of psi, and she moaned just as a vidbot whizzed by.

"Something you two want to share?" Suede was inches from Vin's face.

Armond gave him a shove with psi and the man stepped back, startled. "Easy, hot stuff." He barked out a laugh, and continued through the crowd.

Vin smiled and sighed contentedly. *"Thanks for taking the edge off."*

Armond winked at her. *"My pleasure."*

"I can't wait to see what our prize is," Vin said to Armond. "One winning couple got the title to a resort moon! How cool would it be to own your own moon?"

"I don't need a moon when I have you."

"Awww." She placed her hand on his cheek and blasted a wave of desire through their bond.

Over at the dessert station, Chef Paul had once again outdone himself. An edible star system spanned the table. Suns and planets were made up of bite-sized balls that spun and sparkled. The suns white or yellow, with the planets and moons a dizzying array of ethereal beauty.

Vin plucked a ball from a nearby planet and marveled at its delicacy. It looked as though it was filled with swirling glistening smoke. When she bit into it, a puff of aroma burst forth. The confection melted on her tongue and she moaned with delight. "You have to try one."

Armond leaned over and kissed her hard, sweeping his tongue across hers. "Heavenly."

Vin burst out laughing. "Never had anyone steal food from my mouth before."

"I'm looking forward to a great number of firsts with you."

Suede's voice boomed across the gathering. "And now for the moment we've been waiting for. Can we please have our winning couple on stage!"

"It's about time," Armond said.

Vin grabbed a tiny moon, and they made their way to Suede. The lightning storm to the east was gaining momentum. "Good timing. I'm not liking the looks of that."

They stepped onto the stage and stood where the blondes indicated.

"Always a bittersweet moment when it comes time to say farewell to our contestants," Suede said. "And I'm sure you will all agree, this season did not disappoint! Now, I want to thank our sponsors."

Armond scowled and cursed under his breath.

"Almost there," Vin said as Suede droned on.

Five minutes later, he finally got to the good stuff. "As we already announced, this year's contestants get to keep their ships, and our winners," Suede made a broad gesture at Vin and Armond, "are getting the rights of ownership to a fully operational asteroid mining company."

There was a mixture of cheers and laughs from the audience.

"Seriously? What are we going to do with an asteroid mining company?" Vin was hard pressed not to show her disappointment.

"It's most likely highly lucrative," Armond said.

"It's one of those prizes that could go either way. We'll have to check it out carefully."

Suede made a grand flourish of handing over a golden envelope. Just as Vin accepted the cool foil, the sky to the east flashed a kaleidoscope of colors. A moment later, the lighting orbs began shooting small fireballs in all directions.

The hat of a woman standing directly underneath one of the lights burst into flames. Other tiny fires sparked into life throughout the crowd, and panic erupted.

"That's no electrical storm," Armond said. *"It's time to go."*

They bolted from the stage, but they were stuck. The rooftop only had three access points, all of which were jammed with panicked partygoers.

Vin pulled her com from her bag, "Marty, can you come and pick us up? We're on top of the Octiron building."

"There is an unusual number of aircraft descending upon that location."

"Send the shuttle and do it now," Armond spoke into her unit.

"There's no need to be rude," Marty said.

"Look out!" Vin ducked as a fireball sailed past them.

Armond extended his hand and a pulse of energy spun outward.

"What's that?"

"A shield. It should prevent the flames from penetrating."

"Penetrating, huh?" Vin smiled as she remembered the last time he'd done some penetrating of his own.

A purple ball hit the shield and exploded in a burst of tiny fireballs.

"Oo. Pretty. Find another one."

Vin had to keep her mental shields up, as people were panicking everywhere.

A woman standing in front of them swatted at her head as a ball impacted.

Armond used his psi to stifle the flames.

"Can we kill the light orbs? Stop the projectiles?"

Armond eyed the nearest light. "Perhaps, but it might cause it to explode."

"Good point. Let's not do that."

A fair number of people had made it to safety. Others were being plucked off the roof by a fascinating array of aircraft.

The lights to the east steadied, and the fireballs subsided.

"What is going on over there?"

"I don't know, but I have no desire to stay and find out."

"Marty? Status?" Vin said into her com.

"Your shuttle has one other vehicle in front of it. Please make your way to the south-west corner."

They did as instructed, and spotted the *Galaxy Riders* name on a sleek, metallic four-seater.

"Could have used this a time or two during our race," Vin grumbled. She stepped in as soon as the doors opened, with Armond on her heels.

They were belted in and heading out a moment later.

"Well, that will make for some great viewing," Vin said.

"Speaking of great viewing..." Armond turned to her and brushed his fingers over her breasts.

Love and desire poured across their bond. The flight back to *Galaxy Riders* was quick and entirely too long.

Once the shuttle was secure, they rode the lift to the deck above. The second the doors slid open, the smell of cinnamon permeated the space.

"Orion?" Armond said.

"Congratulations. I am pleased that you won. Separating a bonded couple would bring me no pleasure."

Vin snort laughed. "You aren't the only one." He had their psi buzzing with over-amped pleasure again.

"I have a gift for you, as promised." A glowing blue stone appeared in the air before of them. Armond gently plucked it from space.

"This will allow you to traverse the galaxies as discussed. You will need to come and go from within outlander territories, simply because my friend wishes to know when you are here."

"Can we enter on the fringe? I don't want to start something with them."

"That is both acceptable and advisable."

"Thank you," Vin said. *"Want you in me. Now, Armond."*

"You are welcome." Orion sounded decidedly amused. "Until we meet again, farewell, and enjoy your bond."

The alien's absence was a physical thing. How a disembodied entity had so much presence was a mystery. The effect he had was no mystery, and Vin knew exactly what to do about it. *"Come on, lover. Make me scream."*

"With pleasure."

ALSO BY SABINE PRIESTLEY

Thank you for coming with me to another world! If you enjoyed it, please take a moment and leave a review. Writers live for reviews. Really. A little part of us dies if you don't share the love. For all we know, it might be my left nipple. I don't want to live without that.

XOXO,

Sabine

Curious about Marco and Zara? You can find their story in Sensate - A Stand Alone Novella in the Alien Attachments Series on Amazon.

Want more of the world where Armond and Marco come from? Read on for the first chapter of Alien Attachments.

Sabine writes in multiple genres. You can find all her current work here at www.sabinepriestley.com/sabines-books/

ACKNOWLEDGMENTS

I hope you enjoyed Orion's Gate. If so, *please take a moment and leave a review*. A few words is all it takes. Writers live for reviews. Really. A little part of us dies if you don't share the love. For all we know, it might be my *right nipple*. I don't want to live without that!

Thanks to Candice Phillips Gilmer for the awesome cover, and Laurel Kriegler for the edits.

You can find the entire series of books, all of which stand alone perfectly well, here: www.gspacerace.com

A quick shout out to Cathryn Cade for wrangling the authors! And thanks to the authors who did cross-over scenes with me. Their books are listed below.

Cathryn Cade: Starshadow

JC Hay: Flare

Teresa Noelle Roberts: Explode.

ALIEN ATTACHMENTS BOOK ONE

hapter 1

A DARK-SKINNED MALE AND A TALL BLOND FEMALE DANCED
around each other, bamboo sticks at the ready, waiting for an
opening. Sitting on the warm iron bleachers above, Ian
Cavacent leaned forward in anticipation. The old warehouse
on Cat Island doubled as many things. Tonight, it hosted the
weekly mixed fight competition. The popular event drew
crowds from as far away as Nassau. Humans jostled for a seat
or stood in groups around the improvised, oversized boxing
ring. The target of his interest was the blond woman. He'd
come to watch her for the past few weeks. A friend of his
human support agent, Jared, she fascinated him. He had a
rule to avoid women on the island, but there was something
about this one. She intrigued him. And not for the usual
reasons, either. Yes, she was pretty, beautiful even, but there
was more to it than that.

Jared slid into the seat next to him and handed him a beer. "Dani said you were stalking her."

"I don't stalk." Ian took the plastic cup. "Besides, I wasn't aware she knew I was here."

"Yeah, she told me that too."

Ian took a long pull on the beer. "There's just something odd about her. Maybe it's the way she moves. Her motions aren't practiced, she's constantly off balance, and yet she pulls in win after win. If I didn't know better, I'd say the fights were rigged."

The crowd quieted, and tension rose as the timer ticked down to zero.

Below, the two continued their dance, circling each other. The man lunged and Dani twirled with an awkward step, but still managed to dodge the swing of the bamboo. Sweat dripped into the cleavage of her sports bra and down the small of her back, leaving a dark stain in the fabric. She parried left and right. As usual, her maneuvers were halting and lacked grace.

Ian winced when Jared erupted in one of his booming sneezes. Dani shot an annoyed glance their way. Big mistake. In that fraction of a second, her opponent swung his bamboo. The jagged tip grazed the skin below her left eye before slamming into her wrist. The impact pushed her over the edge. She ducked, nearly fell over, spun around and in a surprisingly fluid movement, sent her opponent's stick flying. The crowd erupted with cheers and jeers for both sides. Money changed hands and the tension evaporated. The two opponents approached each other. Cradling her wrist, Dani declined a handshake. They shared some good-natured words before they left the floor.

Ian's powerful psi allowed him to see a purple mist radiating from her injuries. "That's going to hurt," Ian said.

"Dammit," Jared mumbled, grabbing one of his ever-present tissues. "Can you tell how bad it is?"

"Not yet."

"Well"—Ian swallowed the dregs of his beer—"she may have won, but she's going to be out of commission for awhile. She's not going to be happy with you."

"Yep." Jared wiped his nose. "I best go down and apologize. Come with me? She knows you've been watching. Be kind of weird at this point not to say hello."

A wave of anticipation washed over him. Aside from his three support agents, he limited his involvement with humans to the occasional short-lived affair off the island. Yet his reaction to spending time with this woman surprised him.

"You know I prefer to keep my involvement with humans away from here." Still, he was tempted. On the verge of changing his mind, he sensed a pending communication. "Hold on, incoming message from Marco." Marco was the Earth Protector, or EP, currently on duty. He waited a beat for it to arrive.

We got company, boss. His com relayed the message.

"Apologies are going to have to wait. Someone's paying Earth a visit." Ian said.

Jared followed him out the back door.

DANI WIPED THE SWEAT FROM HER BROW AND FOLLOWED DUGO out of the fight area. Bazillionaire Ian Cavacent and her friend Jared were leaving out the back. Ian always kept to himself, and as far as she knew, never fraternized with the locals except Jared. His recent interest in her sparked an explosion of fantasies. Even better, he seemed the type who would be okay with a "nothing complicated" scenario. And he was hot. Seriously hot, hence the fantasies. She'd love to get him in front of her camera...and a few other places. Those wavy blond locks and smoky green eyes. *Yum. Why haven't you contacted me, Mr. Cavacent?*

Dugo interrupted her musings. "Someone needs to tell Jared to take his allergy meds." He nodded toward her arm. "You okay?"

"I'll be fine." She gave him a good-natured nudge with her other elbow. "You almost got me there."

He took a hand towel off the supplies table and handed it to her. "You're bleeding."

The medic came over and applied antibiotic ointment and a butterfly bandage to her cheek. "You should have that looked at."

"I will," Dani said.

Dugo tossed the towel in the laundry bin. "Glad I missed your eye. Seriously, man. I didn't see you comin'."

"And that's the way it's done," Dani said with all the swagger she could muster. Which was a lot, even with the pain radiating from her wrist.

Dugo laughed. "So what do you say? Have a drink with me?"

"Dugo..."

"Hey," he said, shrugging. "I never see you with no one here. You fly around the world and take your pictures, but this is home. Why you not date anyone?"

"Who says I don't?" Dani could tell by his stance he wasn't buying it. Didn't matter, he didn't have to. It was her business. "Gotta go. Catch ya next time."

~

THE FOLLOWING DAY, AFTER A SWIM ALONG THE BEACH, IAN sat on a barstool across from Jared. Two additional members of his EP team sat on either side of him. They were like night and day. Armond Nolde, white-haired albino, and Marco Dar, dark and swarthy.

"That was no accident last night, boss," Marco said.

"I know." Ian motioned for Jared to pour them some drinks.

After leaving Dani's match, they'd ported off world to the base where their fighters were kept. Humans had no idea their little planet was the focus of increasingly frequent alien attention. It was the EP's job to keep it that way. Last night Torogs attempted to land. During their interception, a team hired by Councilman Gordat Prayda fired on Ian's ship. The Torogs fled, and Prayda's goons claimed mechanical failure of their equipment.

Mechanical failure, like hell. Politics on Sandaria had become increasingly perilous.

Jared poured beers for the three Sandarians and wiped down the already-clean counter.

"Aside from the obvious," the albino Armond said, reaching back to tighten his ubiquitous pony tail, "I find it disturbing Councilman Prayda appears to believe the accidental death of Lord Cavacent's heir and only child would go unpunished."

Armond had a point. "I talked with my father after the incursion last night. He agrees the increase in Torog activity is concerning, but thinks we should stay quiet about the attack on me. The fewer waves we make right now, the better. Let's just try and avoid any further contact with Councilman Prayda's pets."

Marco rapidly tapped his beer glass. "If you'd just let me blast that *crag* last night—"

"The emperor's guards would be all over us," Armond finished.

Ian sensed Marco's rising anger at Armond. The two

rarely saw eye to eye. "At ease." Ian slid Marco's beer away from his tapping finger. He used his psi to calm the man. *I've told you before to stop letting him get under your skin.*

Marco's psi wasn't strong enough to broadcast his thoughts but the release of tension in his shoulders as he took a long pull on his beer was enough for Ian.

Jared, who'd been listening to the exchange, leaned against the bar. "Trouble in paradise?"

Marco snorted.

Ian ignored the reaction and addressed Jared. "Let's just say the empire is a little unstable right now." The concern on Jared's face was clear. "Don't worry too much. Earth shouldn't be involved. Aside from you and the Papallos, Earth can remain blissfully ignorant of the existence of aliens."

Closer to his father's age, Jared bore the appearance of a scruffy old sea captain. He'd worked with his father before Ian took over.

"Where's the new kid?" Jared asked, pouring some mixed nuts into a bowl.

Grinning, Marco grabbed a handful of nuts and shook his head.

"She's getting settled," Ian said. "Has some more unpacking to do. You'll meet her later."

"Marco here said she's height-challenged," Jared said.

Marco held his hand out below shoulder height. It wasn't much, given that he was sitting. "She's a little spitfire."

"Five-foot-four," Ian said.

"With her boots on," Armond added.

Jared raised a bushy eyebrow.

"Just wait till you catch her in action," Ian said. "Unbelievably fast and knows how to use her size to her advantage. Oh, and she's got blazing red hair."

"I have got to see this." Jared blew his nose and shook his head. "You three over six-foot, and Little Red Riding Hood."

Ian laughed. "An odd picture all right. It works, though. She nailed the trial and has total psi-control over her ship. Never once went to manual."

"So, what do you think the Torogs were coming for?" Jared asked.

"The usual," Ian said. "Hunting humans or going after carnium."

Jared stacked more glasses behind the bar. "That's the stuff you use to go all faster than light, right?"

Ian found Jared's vernacular to be a continuing source of entertainment. "Been taking notes?"

"I work for aliens. I'm always taking notes." Jared leaned back against the bar and crossed his arms. "Third time this week Torogs have hit our radar. What's going on?"

"I wish we knew," Ian said.

Jared remained silent for a moment. "You know, boss. I don't like the idea of Earth not having you guys around. Don't go gettin' yourself killed."

"I don't plan to. My father thinks the emperor doesn't have long. The problem is, no one knows who or what will take his place. Until we know that, we just have to ride it out." Ian's psi registered the approaching vehicle before he heard the crunch of tires on the crushed-shell gravel outside. Desire pulsed through him. "Well, well. Looks like we've got company. Sounds like Ms. Standich herself." Ian took a beat to enjoy the sensations she induced.

"She the one you're stalking?" Marco said.

Ian scowled at him. "I'm not stalking her."

"Whatever you say, boss." Marco pointed a finger at Jared. "He said it."

Jared plucked a nut out of the dish and flicked it at Marco.

The nut stopped in mid air, a few inches from Marco's face and spun around for a moment. Marco flicked his finger. The nut shot through the air and bounced off Jared's head, causing him to burst out laughing.

A moment later, the massive wood plank that made up the front entrance creaked open grudgingly. Sand scraped against the floor. The sliding doors at the back of the bar stood wide open, and the cross breeze pulled at Dani's blond hair as she struggled with the weight.

"When," she said, clutching a white hat and beach bag, "are you going to fix this thing?" She held her right wrist close to her chest. Slipping through the opening, she turned to use her rear to push the beast closed. She gave a mighty shove with her ass. The door gave more than expected and she let out a short squeak as she tried to regain her balance.

Graceful as always, Ian thought.

"Thanks for your help last night, by the way." Dani glared at Jared.

Ian stifled a laugh.

Waves of purple radiated from her arm and the left side of her face. She wore large, dark sunglasses that hid the injury to her eye, but her wrist was visibly bruised and swollen.

Jared rushed around the bar and gave the door a shove. "What can I say? My allergies never stop. You gotta learn not to be distracted."

"Hold it in next time."

"Sure, kid." Jared kicked at the bottom of the door, which finally clicked shut.

Ian was surprised by the obvious closeness of the relationship, but then he never stuck around when locals came into the bar. Until now.

"So?" Dani said, placing her bag and hat on a bar stool not

far from Ian and his EPs. "When are you going to fix that thing?"

"Fix it? Why? Keeps the tourists down to a minimum."

"You own a bar on the beach. Aren't you supposed to want tourists?"

Jared shrugged. "I'm good with the ones I get from the hotel"—he indicated a path leading up a slight hill—"and the few wanderers."

Dani gazed at the beach beyond the small patio and sighed. "You do have a slice of heaven here."

Jared poured some nuts into a bowl and slid them across to her. "I don't think you've formally met my friends here." He indicated the team. "This is Armond, Marco and 'course you know about Ian. Guys, this here is Dani."

They exchanged greetings and Dani focused on Ian. "Been enjoying my fights, Mr. Cavacent?" She smiled with her striking blue eyes.

Jared coughed loudly.

Ian was sure the word "stalker" was buried in the cough somewhere. He decided to ease up on his usual role of arrogant millionaire. He needed to find out why she captivated him so. "Call me Ian, and yes, I have been enjoying your fights. You have an unusual technique."

Dani scoffed. "Lack thereof, you mean." She removed her sunglasses and revealed a nasty gash below her left eye. Dark bruises surrounded the puffy wound.

"Ouch." Jared leaned in for a closer inspection. "At least you won."

Dani set the glasses down. "Yeah, well it's going to be awhile before I can compete again. I figure you owe me some drinks in the meantime."

"Suppose that's only fair."

Fascinating purple swirls worked their way up to her shoulder and out from her cheek. The color was deep and rich, meaning she was in a great deal of pain. That, or she had an unusually high tolerance for it.

Dani dug around her bag with her left hand and pulled out an insulated Tervis cup. "Rum and coke, please." She slid the cup over to Jared.

"Want some ice for that wrist? And maybe your face?" he asked.

"No, thanks."

Jared set her drink down while she gathered up her bag and put her sunglasses back on.

"Why thank you kindly, sir," she said with an exaggerated southern accent. "I always rely upon the kindness of strangers."

Jared bowed. "Anything for you, Miss Scarlett."

"Boys." She gave a nod and headed for the path leading to the hotel pool.

Ian waited until she was out of earshot. "She moves like a cat."

The men watched as she tripped and sloshed her drink onto the path.

"A clumsy cat," Marco said, finishing his beer. "That's it for me. I can't take this humidity. I'll check in with you later, boss." He stood. "Thanks, Jared."

"I too, have had enough of this damp climate of yours." Armond said, getting to his feet. "I'll report in this evening." He followed Marco out.

Jared sneezed. "That's why you selected this place, isn't it?"

Ian didn't answer, just grinned. "How long have you known her?" He indicated the direction Dani had taken.

"Years," Jared said around his tissue. "Her aunt took her in when her parents died in a plane crash. She was only fifteen or sixteen at the time. I used to let her sweep up around the bar in exchange for sodas. Got the feeling she needed the company. Anyway, auntie spends most of her time in New York these days. Dani keeps the house going when she's not off freelancing for Vogue or some other slick rag."

"Journalist?"

"Photographer. She's good too, if you like that sort of thing." Jared wiped his nose again. "Personally, I prefer landscapes and animals to pretty humans." Jared popped a few peanuts into his mouth. "She's in pain."

"That woman, my friend, is in a world of hurt," Ian agreed.

"Think maybe you could help her out?"

Ian finished off his beer. "You know how I am about getting involved with locals."

"She's good people, boss. Besides you don't have to get involved." Jared made quotes with his fingers around the last words. "I've never seen her with anyone. Losing your folks at such a young age, I suppose it can mess you up. Just tell her you know some techniques to help with the pain."

Ian cast another look at the retreating woman. "Why are you so concerned? Is there something I should know about you two?"

Jared harrumphed and crossed his arms. "I'm old enough to be her dad."

"So?"

"I'll admit, I have a soft spot for her, but it's more like a daughter. Like I said, she's good people."

Ian couldn't deny his attraction to her, and he was curious to see if he could figure out why he found her so appealing. Probably those blue eyes. *I'll talk to her for a while. She'll have nothing to say, and I'll get her out of my system.* "Fine. But just enough to ease her pain. I can't do more, obviously."

"Obviously. Thanks, boss. Hey, when you get back, I'll buy you a beer."

"That's real generous, considering I own the place."

Jared chuckled and ate another handful of peanuts.

~

DANI HAD FINALLY GOTTEN HERSELF SITUATED ON THE RAFT, her drink within reach on the deck, when she noticed Ian heading her way. A deep thrill rippled through her and she bit her lip. The pool area was empty except an old couple eating ice cream at the far end.

Ian sat next to her cup, and dangled his legs in the water. Nice, muscular legs.

"Hello again," he said.

"Ian." Dani nodded in greeting.

"I'm guessing you're in a fair amount of pain right now."

"Nothing I can't handle." Where was he going with this?

"If you're interested, I'm proficient in an ancient Chinese art of pain management."

Dani tilted her hat to get a better view. "Seriously?" She'd heard some lines in her time, but that had to be the cheesiest.

"Seriously." He shrugged and took a sip of her drink.

Dani huffed and scowled at him. "You better not drink it all or you'll have to get me another one." His smoky green eyes were an intriguing contrast to his olive skin. The way he looked at her made her body tingle. "How exactly does this Chinese voodoo work?"

Ian pushed off the side and into the water with a smile on his face. "Certain places on the body can be manipulated to ease pain and do other things like lower blood pressure." He stood next to her, causing a slight wake to bob the raft up and down.

"Hmm...I don't know."

"Really? Jared's worried about you and I promised I'd help."

Dani glanced back toward the bar. She couldn't see Jared from here, but she knew he'd be worried. It's what he did under all that gruffness. When she looked back, she found Ian's gaze had shifted to somewhere south of her eyes. A flood of pleasure washed over her at the thought of his lips on her breast.

She cleared her throat.

Ian smiled at her with a crooked grin.

The thrill from earlier boiled over to something far less manageable. *Wow. This is some serious attraction.* "Um, precisely where and how will you be manipulating me?"

Ian laughed. "I assure you my intentions are honorable."

Well, that was disappointing. She tilted her head. If he didn't feel the same attraction right now, she'd eat her bikini. "Go ahead then. Let's see what you can do." She pulled her hat down over her face and leaned back.

The raft rocked in the water as he moved behind her. He lightly touched her injured arm sending a zap of euphoria through her. *Wow.*

His fingers slowly trailed up each of her arms and the tension in her core rose with it. As he reached the base of her neck, she said a little prayer he'd be open to a friends-with-benefits situation. His hands settled on her shoulder muscles and pressed harder. A bolt of pleasure shot through her. *This is insane.* She couldn't slow her breathing. He was no where near her private bits, yet it was as if...

Ian ran his thumbs up the cords in her neck.

She caught her breath as the intensity increased. *No way.* Her body tensed as pleasure exploded, leaving her motionless as the incredible sensation rolled outward to her fingers and toes. *Holy shit.*

~

Ian drew his fingers along the top of Dani's shoulders, enjoying the buzz her silky smooth skin created.

Her body shivered, causing his psi to ripple through him. *Interesting.*

He gently probed along the muscles to find the right spot.

Dani let out a long sigh and relaxed into his hands.

He found it odd he'd have such intense chemistry with a human. He closed his eyes and reached out with his psi. Her cheek possessed only a flesh wound so he dampened the nerve endings to stop the pain. Next he moved to her wrist where he found a hairline fracture. He focused his psi and mended the bone, leaving most of the bruised tissue and muscle, but again dampened the nerve endings. A minute passed before Ian realized something was off. His psi buzzed with an energy he'd never experienced before.

Dani's breathing quickened.

He was about to let go when a blast of psi tore into him. The sheer force was astonishing. He nearly flung her behind him, before he realized it *was* her.

Not possible. Humans don't have psi. Unable to resist, he explored further. Like a Sandarian child, her psi was unrefined and clearly not under control. He should let go, but like a moth to a flame, he delved deeper. And deeper still. The magnitude floored him. She could very well be as strong as he.

This had the potential to change everything. If people on his planet found out, his family could lose all rights to this world. Rights to both the carnium and their protectorship of Earth. Humans could never defend themselves against the aliens who would come looking for an easy grab at the coveted mineral. With the unrest of the empire, it might be years before another protectorship could be effectively established and agreed upon. By then, Goddess knew, how much damage would have been done.

A human with psi. It made no sense. His family had been protecting Earth for generations. Never had a human been found with psi. He'd been with a number of women, and never had there been an inkling. He needed to discuss this with his father. He began to pull back. As though in response to his leaving, her psi pulsed and pleasure unlike anything he'd ever imagined washed though him. His body and psi buzzed with the intense energy. Stronger and stronger it grew. He drew a deep breath, riding the wave of pure ecstasy.

Almost as if—*Holy Goddess.* Ian slammed the connection closed and staggered back. His heart pounded in his chest. He stared at his hands as though they belonged to someone else. *My psi-mate?* The pleasure slowly subsided. He wanted more, needed more. *Mother Goddess help me.*

Chairs scrapped across the pool deck and snapped him out of his reverie. He threw a glance over his shoulder. The old couple prepared to leave. The man winked at Ian, then said something to the woman that made her laugh.

He returned his attention to Dani. She inhaled quickly as if she'd been holding her breath. He stood a moment longer, torn between staying, because he wanted to, and returning to Sandaria to talk with his father. Duty won. He whirled around, slicing through the water.

She called after him but he didn't respond.

What did I just do?

~

DANI COUGHED AS WATER SPLASHED OVER HER FACE FROM IAN'S abrupt departure. She jerked to a sitting position. She'd been momentarily paralyzed, and it freaked her out. The movement sent pulses of pleasure rippling through her. *Holy crap, that was amazing.* "Hey, what was that? Ian?" She spun around to find him nearly at the steps. "Ian!"

He bolted out of the water and headed back to the bar, dripping wet.

The photographer in her couldn't help but analyze the scene. *Damn, he does wet really well.* Dani wiped the water from her eyes and looked around for her hat. *Crap.* She reached over and plucked the soggy mess off the surface of the water. Plopping it on her head, she sighed as the water-logged rim flopped over her face. *Great.* She shook the hat out a few times and stopped mid-swing.

What the... Slowly, she put the hat back on her head and held up her injured hand. She flexed her fingers and bent her wrist back and forth. The tendons were stiff and still looked like hell, but there was no pain. Swinging her legs off the lounge, she slid into the waist-deep water. Submerging her hand, she drew her palm back and forth under the surface. Still no pain. *What in the world did he do?*

Dani got out of the pool, gathered up her bag and drink and hurried down the path after him. She flexed her pain-free wrist the whole way.

Jared stood behind the bar, filling salt shakers.

"Where'd Ian go?"

"Said he had to run."

"Yeah, literally. I want to talk to him about this pressure point thing." Dani sat across from him.

"Pressure point?"

"You know, the pain thing."

"Oh yeah, how'd it go? Pretty cool, huh?" Jared screwed the lid on a shaker.

"I guess. I mean the results are great. Unbelievable really, but the effect—" Dani stopped herself. What was she going to do? Tell Jared she'd just had some freak pleasure event? As if. "I just can't believe how effective this pressure point thing is." She slid her empty cup over to Jared. "Can I have another rum and coke, please? Mr. Personality sloshed water in mine."

Jared put down the shaker. "Sure. I take it you're feeling better?" He rinsed out the Tervis cup and made another drink.

"I'll say. He's got a nice touch, I'll give him that." *There's an understatement.* "But as soon as he finished, he bolted from the pool. Swamped me with his wake. Got my new hat wet."

"Really?"

"Yeah, and check this out." Dani held up her wrist and twisted it around. "What the—even the bruising is going away now, look."

Jared leaned in for a closer inspection and frowned. His eyes moved from her wrist to her face. "Take your glasses off, Dani."

She did as he asked.

"Oh, dear."

"What? What's wrong?" She reached up and probed the gash under her eye. The skin felt like a month-old scar. "Jared, what's going on?"

~

If you liked the opening of Alien Attachments, you can grab a copy today!
Alien Attachments